MURDER
— OF THE —
BRIDE

A Rex Graves Mystery

MURDER
— OF THE —
BRIDE

C. S. CHALLINOR

MIDNIGHT INK
WOODBURY, MINNESOTA

Book design by Donna Burch
Cover design and photo illustration by Kevin R. Brown
Cover photo images: Church © iStockphoto.com/Max Homand,
    Crow © iStockphoto.com/Daniel Cardiff, Raven © iStockphoto
    .com/Frank Leung
Editing by Connie Hill

Midnight Ink, an imprint of Llewellyn Worldwide Ltd.

ISBN 978-1-61793-943-3

Midnight Ink
Llewellyn Worldwide Ltd.
2143 Wooddale Drive
Woodbury, MN 55125-2989

Printed in the United States of America

DEDICATION

In memory of Mark Challinor

CAST OF MAIN CHARACTERS

Rex Graves—Scottish barrister and amateur sleuth

Helen d'Arcy—Rex's fiancée, a school counselor in Derby

Reverend Alfred Snood—vicar of All Saints' Church in Aston-on-Trent

Detectives Lucas and Dartford—of the Derbyshire Constabulary

PC Dimley—rookie constable

PC Perrin—young policeman, going places

On the Bride's Side

Polly Newcombe—the less than lily-white bride

Victoria Newcombe—bride's pretentious mother

Gwendolyn Jones—bride's aunt on her father's side

Amber Tate—maid of honor and Polly's best friend

Meredith Matthews—bride's friend from school who lives in London

Reggie Cox—Meredith's sartorially flamboyant boyfriend

Bobby Carter—Newcombe family solicitor

Roger Litton—Polly's former home economics teacher at Oakleaf Comprehensive

Diana Litton—history teacher married to Roger Litton

On the Groom's Side

Timothy Thorpe—a well-intentioned groom with a weak chin

Mabel Thorpe—the groom's fussy and overprotective mother

Dudley Thorpe—the groom's womanizing twin and best man

Donna Thorpe—Dudley's disenchanted wife

Tom Willington—the groom's boss at the accounting firm

Jocelyn Willington—Tom Willington's bossy wife

Clive Rutherford—Timmy's former mathematics teacher and Helen's ex-boyfriend
Jasmina Patel—Clive's stunning date
Jeremy Walker—Timmy's friend from accounting school
Elaine Price—Jeremy's drippy girlfriend

Staff

Stella and Lydia Pembleton—the caterers
Rachel Pembleton—Lydia's daughter, waitress
Harry Futuro—a.k.a. DJ Smoothie

Mrs. Victoria Newcombe
requests the pleasure of the company of

Ms. Helen d'Arcy & Guest

at the marriage of her daughter
Miss Polly Anne
to
Mr. Timothy P. Thorpe

At
All Saints' Church in Aston-on-Trent

on
Saturday, 29th of May at 11 am

followed by a wedding reception at
Newcombe Court, Newcombe, Derbyshire

RSVP…

"THE DARLING BUDS OF MAY"

NOT A VERY AUSPICIOUS day for a wedding, Rex thought as he looked out Helen's bedroom window. A drizzly gray day beckoned feebly, and windy gusts rapped the branches of the willow tree against the panes of double glazing. Evidently, May in Derbyshire was no more predictable than May back home in Scotland, and Rex felt sorry for the bride and groom who would be setting out on a new life together this very day.

Wrapped in his flannel dressing gown, Helen entered the room with a tray and placed it between them on the bed before burrowing her feet under the covers. "You must have brought the cold weather down from Edinburgh," she said. "I had to put the central heating back on."

"It was fine weather in Scotland when I left yesterday afternoon. Helen, you should have let me make breakfast."

"I felt like spoiling you. I tried to make your eggs the way you like them—soft-boiled, but not too runny. And the marmalade is homemade, courtesy of Roger Litton, the Home Ec teacher at my school."

She proceeded to pour tea into two blue mugs. "I hope the rain will clear up for the wedding today."

"And for our hiking trip." A keen walker and nature-lover, Rex was looking forward to their excursion into the Peak District the following day.

"I do feel sorry for Polly and Timothy," his fiancée remarked. "But I think it's an indoor reception. Anyway, it may still turn out sunny."

"You are the eternal optimist, Helen." Rex took a more pragmatic view of British weather: be prepared and always take a brolly. He cracked the shell of his egg with the back of his spoon, sprinkled on some salt and pepper, and dipped a buttered strip of toast into the thick warm yolk.

"Perfect," he complimented Helen on the consistency of the egg and, noticing she was not eating anything, asked, "Not hungry?"

"I have to fit into my suit," she explained.

"Och, it's not like you're the bride. All eyes will be on Polly."

"Including yours?"

"That's not what I meant."

"I know. You're just trying to be helpful." She deposited a conciliatory peck on his cheek. "I can't believe Polly is getting married," she went on dreamily. "But Timmy ended up doing all right for himself, considering he was such a sickly child and missed a lot of school."

"You said he was an accountant?"

"Yes, at quite a prestigious firm." Helen shook her head in disbelief. "Seems like just yesterday Polly was in my office crying and carrying on. That girl had so many problems."

"Were they childhood sweethearts?"

"Oh, no," Helen said, refilling their mugs. "Timmy was bullied mercilessly at school. Polly, on the other hand . . . well, let's just say she was very popular with the boys. While Timmy was being picked on in the playground, she was kissing all and sundry behind the bicycle shed. After she dropped out, we heard she was going with an undesirable character from Aston. So when we got the invitation to the wedding, we at the school were all rather surprised—and touched. And her mother is ecstatic."

"Have you met Mrs. Newcombe?"

"Yes, and she's perfectly dreadful."

Rex shot Helen a look, his spoon suspended midway to his mouth. "That's the first time I've ever heard you speak an unkind word aboot anybody," he said, his Scottish accent betrayed in the "aboot."

"I know, it's totally uncharitable of me, but you'll find out for yourself. They live in a Victorian Folly—one of those whimsical places built by people with more money than sense. Anyway, the headmaster used to call Mrs. Newcombe in to his office most weeks to discuss Polly's behaviour—her smoking on school grounds, the truancy, and so on, so I got to know her quite well. No dad in the picture, you see. He disappeared, quite mysteriously, while Polly was still very young."

"An only child?"

"Yes, and only an aunt in the family."

"It must be gratifying to know you had a positive influence on Polly's life." Rex checked his watch. "What time do we have to get going?"

"By ten."

An hour later, they were getting ready to leave the house. Standing in front of the hallway mirror, Rex spruced up his ginger whiskers with a brush of his fingers. The silk tie Helen had surprised him with was the same cornflower blue as her tailored suit, and the exact shade of her eyes. He leaned toward the glass. Did the tie clash with his hair? No, of course not; Helen had perfect taste in all things.

"You look amazing," he told her reflection behind him.

Her ears beneath the blond chignon revealed the swan earrings he had bought for her when they first met, that Christmas at Swanmere Manor, the location of his first private murder case.

"You don't look half bad yourself." She adjusted the pink silk carnation in the buttonhole of his charcoal gray jacket.

The boutonniere had been sent with the invitation. The card, a pink affair with scalloped edges and embossed in gold script, currently reposed against the clock on the living room mantelpiece. Rex had an inkling a leitmotif of pink would run through the day's proceedings. He just hoped there would be a lavish banquet. He already felt peckish, in spite of the breakfast he had consumed. "How many people will be there?" he inquired.

"Polly said it would be a small reception for family and close friends, and a few teachers from the school, including Clive."

"As in Clive, your old boyfriend?" Hmm ... Rex didn't quite know how he felt about Helen's ex-beau attending the wedding. Emotions tended to run high at such occasions, especially when everybody had too much to drink. Still, it might be interesting to finally meet the mathematics teacher and see if he was as boring as Rex imagined him to be.

"Yes, Clive will be there," Helen said lightly, "as will the Littons. Roger was Polly's Home Ec teacher and sort of took her under his wing. Diana teaches history."

Rex speculated anew about the tie. Undoubtedly, Helen was keen to present him in the best possible light to her friends—and to Clive, whose attendance she had flagrantly omitted to mention when she invited him to her protégée's nuptials two months ago.

He watched as she checked the locks on the windows and the bolt on the back door. "I didn't know you were so security conscious," he remarked.

"I'm not, usually, but there's been a spate of burglaries in the county. Not that I have a lot in the way of valuables, as you know. Mostly, it's big places in outlying areas that have been targeted."

Rex carried the gift for the bride and groom outside, a cut-glass fruit bowl that Helen had purchased. He couldn't understand why a young couple would require a gargantuan fruit bowl, and privately considered a toaster a more practical present for two people setting up house for the first time together.

He held his black umbrella over Helen's head as they started down the path to the driveway, at the same time attempting to keep droplets of rain off the gift's white and silver wrapping. Juggling gift and brolly, he opened the driver's door of her old blue Renault, which was marginally roomier than his Mini Cooper. Environmental concerns aside, he would not have opted for such a compact car had he anticipated frequent trips from Edinburgh to Derby. Next time he would take the train and save himself the leg-cramping 250 mile drive.

Installed in the passenger seat, gift perched on his knees, he pulled a map from the door pocket and located Aston-on-Trent on the outskirts of Derby, neighboring the canal village of Shardlow. Helen set the windshield wipers in motion and reversed into Barley Close, a cul-de-sac lined with 1930s semi-detached red brick homes, the sodden front lawns and early summer flowerbeds as forlorn as a lover stood up in the rain.

Definitely not an auspicious day for a wedding.

R.I.P.
———

THE RENAULT TURNED INTO a winding country lane edged with glistening hawthorn and, after half a mile, entered the village of Aston-on-Trent. Several homes appeared originally to have been farm houses, though many of more modern aspect had been added as the village grew into a commuter center, situated as it was just six miles southeast of Derby.

From Manor Farm Road, Helen exited onto The Green, where a half-timbered public house displayed the words "The Malt Shovel" in brass letters on its white wall. To make the point, a hanging sign depicted a man in a leather apron digging into a pile of malt. Rex made a mental note, fond as he was of pubs.

"This road loops around the back of the church," Helen told Rex. "Hopefully we'll find a parking space."

"Do we have time for a pint if the pub's open?"

Helen glanced, frowning, at the dashboard clock. "The wedding service starts at ten-thirty. If I can find a spot near the church, I won't have to walk far in these shoes."

Ahead of them, the square Norman tower of All Saints' rose above the treetops beyond the tip of the village green.

"I could drop you off and park the car," Rex suggested. And then get a quick pint, he forbore from adding aloud.

"I'd prefer we arrive together. In any case, most pubs in England don't open until eleven."

Rex conceded defeat. It was Helen's day, after all. "I hope they have beer at the reception," he contented himself by saying as he gazed longingly over his shoulder at the pub.

Helen had started to reply when she exclaimed in triumph, "Oh, look, someone's just leaving," and edged the Renault in between two other cars on the street. "We'll leave the gift here. Newcombe Court is a few miles from the village, so we'll be driving over to the reception."

"Right-oh." Rex wondered how long the church service would last, not having attended a wedding in decades. Had that been his own wedding? No, there had been the marriage in Edinburgh of the son of a legal colleague some years ago, a full-blown traditional affair—bagpipes, kilts, swords, and all.

He levered himself out of the car and, opening the door for Helen, shielded her under his brolly as they approached the church. The churchyard wall was linked by an oak lychgate— "lic" meaning corpse in old English, as Rex had once informed himself; the covered gate serving in olden days to shelter the coffin and pallbearers while they waited for the priest to perform the burial service. Beneath the rafters of the pitched tile roof huddled a group of gussied-up couples equipped with an assortment of umbrellas, temporarily furled.

Now that he had an unobstructed view of All Saints', Rex recognized it as a beautifully preserved example of a Midlands parish church, begun in Saxon times, with the tower, buttresses, battlements, and four Victorian pinnacles added down the ages, and incorporating the straight lines of the Perpendicular period in between. Layered with history, the brown-gray edifice gave an overall appearance of something out of a Gothic melodrama as it brooded against the gloomy late morning sky.

The clock face beneath the Norman window in the north wall of the tower pointed to one minute before the half hour. A moment later, a six-bell peal rang out, scattering a flock of thirteen ravens from the battlements. The last of the guests hurried down the churchyard path amid ancient headstones embedded in the wet grass and streamed through the pointed arched doorway of the porch.

As Rex and Helen entered the short nave, a po-faced young woman in a frilly pink dress handed them a sheet edged in gold. She ushered them toward the pews to the left of the central aisle, which had already filled up with the bride-to-be's family and friends.

Rex looked around for someone who might fit his mental picture of Clive, the mathematics teacher, but most of the thirty or so guests had their backs to him, having arrived earlier. The traffic out of Derby that Saturday morning had been surprisingly heavy and slowed down by rain.

Helen waved to a woman in a lilac outfit and large straw hat seated four rows ahead beside a bald man in a brown jacket. "That's Diana Litton and her husband," she told Rex.

Mrs. Litton, who wore translucent pink-framed glasses and a flirty shade of lipstick, waved back with enthusiasm. Rex thought she looked like she might be good company.

"There's loads of history in this church," Helen proceeded to inform him. "Diana brought a class here on a field trip, and I tagged along as a helper." She pointed to the front of the side aisle, separated from the eight rows of blue-padded pews by an arcade of stone arches set atop heavy, round pillars. "Over by the organ is an alabaster tomb from the fifteenth century bearing the effigy of a local landowner in a round cap and gown with his wife lying beside him, each with a dog at their feet."

The crouching dogs' extremities had partially crumbled away. Carved in bas-relief on the chest tomb below, a series of angels held shields engraved with coats of arms.

"The couple is united in death," Helen whispered. "Romantic, don't you think?"

"Only if they weren't going at it hammer and tongs in married life," Rex whispered back. "Perhaps she never let him go down to the ale house."

Helen feigned an exasperated sigh, but further discussion was forestalled by the opening chords to Wagner's "Wedding March" booming sonorously from a robust set of organ pipes. The muted conversations ceased. Heads turned toward the back of the church as a hugely pregnant bride sailed down the oxblood red carpet on the arm of a stout man, hair resembling white plumage backcombed over his head.

"That's Bobby Carter, a family friend, standing in for Polly's dad," Helen murmured in Rex's ear.

Rex was more transfixed by Polly, whose frothy white dress flaunted a generous bosom while doing little to conceal her advanced condition. The old playground chant, *"Here comes the bride, forty inches wide!"* flowed unbidden to his mind as the organ music played valiantly on from the side aisle.

"Here comes the blushing bride," chorused a hushed but resonant male voice from the pews.

"Blushing, ha!" rejoined a female.

Why, Rex wondered, had the couple left the nuptials so late? If they had been waiting for a May wedding in the hope of fine weather, they must be sadly disappointed.

A chaplet of pink roses crowned Polly's twelve-foot veil, the train held aloft by a pair of giggling teenage girls in ankle-length pink frills. The sullen young woman who had distributed the service sheets scattered petals from a wicker basket in the wake of the bridal procession.

Rex inched closer to the aisle, curious to see the waiting groom-to-be. Two young men stood at the foot of the chancel steps. One, dressed in a dove-gray three-piece suit, came across as highly impressed with himself, judging by his cocky attitude and dark, gel-spiked hair. The fair, lanky youth beside him wore a loose-fitting white tuxedo and had a pinched look about him. The disparity between Polly's fecund girth and the groom's rail thinness became all the more evident when they took their place together before the vicar.

"Timmy looks like he's about to faint," Helen said standing on tiptoe for a better view of the proceedings.

"If Polly doesn't give birth first," Rex replied. "She's enormous. Are we coming back later today for the christening?"

Helen made a heroic effort to compose her face as the solemn occasion dictated, but Rex found himself greatly entertained by the spectacle, especially since the snowy-haired vicar in his pristine white surplice was straight out of central casting.

Reverend Alfred Snood introduced himself in a quavering voice amplified by a microphone and welcomed the assembly to the venerable sanctity of All Saints' Church which, he said, had officiated over many marriages down the centuries. He led the audience in prayer and enjoined them to sing "All Things Bright and Beautiful." Those in the pews rose as the organ struck the first note, lending their voices to the choir sequestered in the polished oak stalls of the chancel, chastely adorned with white floral arrangements.

Rex sang along, looking out over the bare heads and dressy hats. Watery light penetrated the clerestory windows and jewel-toned stained glass, failing, however, to dissipate the stony chill of the old church.

"In the presence of God, Father, Son, and Holy Spirit, we have come together to witness the marriage of Polly and Timothy, to pray for God's blessing on them, to share their joy and to celebrate their love ..."

Settling back in his pew, Rex closed his eyes and listened with vague attention to the vicar addressing the congregation from his elevated stance before the betrothed. "I am required to ask anyone present who knows a reason whereby these two persons may not be joined in lawful matrimony to speak now or forever hold your peace," Reverend Snood announced.

A tomblike silence descended in what Rex could only describe as a pregnant pause, ending at length when the reverend asked the couple if either of *them* knew of a reason why they could not lawfully marry. A buzz-like mumbling arose among the guests on both sides of the aisle. Rex glanced quizzically at Helen, who shrugged in surprise.

When neither bride nor groom spoke, Reverend Snood inquired of Timmy if he would take Polly to be his wife, love her, comfort her, honour and protect her, and, forsaking all others, be faithful to her as long as they both should live; and received a timorous "I will." Polly, asked the same question regarding Timmy, responded in kind.

Lambs to the slaughter, Rex mused, wondering about the future in store for these two. They seemed so young to be getting wed—about the same age as his son, now attending college in Florida. Rex's own marriage had been curtailed when his wife Fiona died of breast cancer six years previously. A lump formed in his throat.

By the time he came to from his reminiscences, it was time to sing "Morning Has Broken," a hymn he particularly liked and rendered with great gusto in his bass-baritone. The reverend invited the couple facing him to join hands and make their vows. Rex surreptitiously glanced at his watch. He was getting hungry, and his earlier longing for beer had quadrupled in intensity.

"Who is the best man?" he asked Helen as the individual in the dove-gray morning suit swaggered forward to give the groom the ring, while Polly accepted hers from the maid of honor.

"That's Dudley, Timmy's twin."

"Twin?" Rex echoed in astonishment. The two men could not have appeared more different. Though not as tall as his brother, Dudley was broader across the shoulders and more muscular. He exuded vigor and virility, and there could be no denying that his features, while coarser than Timmy's, held a certain handsomeness that, along with his confident demeanor, could not fail to appeal to women.

"Attractive, isn't he?" Helen said, confirming Rex's assessment. "I wonder where his wife is." Craning her neck, she scanned the opposite side of the aisle. "Don't see her, or the kids. Oh, look, there's Clive. Ooh, he brought a date."

Rex discerned a trace of surprise—or was it disappointment?—in Helen's voice, and followed her gaze to where a couple sat close together in the right-hand pews. They were several rows forward, and he could only make out the back of Clive's head and, beside him, a pair of bare shoulders loosely draped with a silk shawl. The poor lass must be freezing, he reflected. Jet-black hair snaked down her back. The effect of hair, skin, and shimmering silk was nothing short of exotic. A silver hoop dangling from a pixie ear sparkled in the dim lamp light as she leaned in to address her companion.

"Looks like Clive did all right for himself," Rex murmured to Helen, who continued to gaze across at them in bemusement.

"I'll say."

Their attention reverted toward the altar when the vicar warbled into his microphone, "I now proclaim that they are husband and wife." Joining the right hands of the newlywed couple, he declared, "Those whom God has joined together, let no one put asunder!"

Amen, thought Rex.

THE MERRY WIDOW
FROM WALES

THE SUN MADE A brief, albeit halfhearted, appearance while the newlyweds and family members posed in front of the lychgate for photos, while the bridesmaids shivered in their pink gowns, awaiting their turn. Helen pulled a digital camera from her handbag and directed it at the group, the focal point of which was Mrs. Newcombe.

An undeniably handsome woman, she wore an off-white linen sheath dress and matching hat, its brim as wide as a satellite dish. Beside her, Bobby Carter, who had walked Polly up the aisle, grinned heartily, ruddy-faced beneath his plume of white hair growing up and out from his scalp like porcupine quills. And that must be Timmy's mother, Rex surmised as he watched a diminutive woman in a beige suit and cloche hat fuss over her son.

"Now, where did you put your inhaler, Timmy?"

"I have it, Mum."

"Are you sure now? You look a bit peaky. Did you remember your Tums?"

A strong resemblance existed between them, Timmy having inherited his mother's weak chin, though fortunately for him, not the two whiskers sprouting from a large mole located in its center. Dudley owed her his dark hair and thin, beaky nose.

"Timmy, you're perspiring. Let me just blot your face a bit for the wedding photos."

"I'm cold, not hot," he told his mother in a raspy voice, swatting her off as he would an annoying bluebottle fly. Since Mrs. Thorpe was considerably shorter than her son, her ineffectual attempts to ready him for the camera proved quite comical to Rex as he watched the proceedings.

He thought it just as well the bride's mother had made the wedding arrangements, even if she did appear to enjoy tooting her own horn about it, telling all and sundry what a feat it had been organizing the event. In fact, Victoria Newcombe barely paused for breath except to smile in superior fashion for the professional photographer, a disheveled man in a suit.

"The flowers, transport, caterers, music, photography and video, not to mention the wedding dress!" Mrs. Newcombe expatiated to her immediate circle of guests in haughty tones where the flat vowels of the region were all but absent. "Almost fifteen thousand pounds, just for this small affair. The church part was the least expensive item, can you believe! But I only have the one child and I wanted to give her a proper send-off. Thank goodness Mabel is paying for the honeymoon. She fixed them up on a package tour to Majorca." The way Mrs. Newcombe said this denoted how common she thought the destination. "But, of course, Mabel is on her own, like me, and it's the best she could do under the circumstances." She bestowed a gracious smile on the small woman in beige, who now smoothed Dudley's jacket in preparation for his group photo, while the rest of the guests waited, anxiously gazing up at the sky.

"Give over!" he snapped, adjusting his own tie. "It's Cry-Baby Timmy needs his nose wiping."

"Where's Donna?" Helen asked Dudley, tactfully coming to Timmy's rescue. Or perhaps Dudley's, since the new groom looked ready to lunge at his twin.

"Kids came down with the flu, and Donna had to stay home with them. But I couldn't miss my baby brother's wedding, could I?" he declared, following up with a seductive wink at Helen.

"I thought you and Timmy were twins," Rex interjected, suddenly taking exception to Dudley's dark designer stubble and fluorescent white teeth.

"Came out first, didn't I?"

Probably always came first, Rex decided. Dudley's aggressive, rhetorical-question style of conversation was beginning to grate, and Rex distanced himself.

Helen gestured to the maid of honor. "Amber, can you move in a bit closer so I can fit everyone in my view finder?"

This was the girl who had strewn rose petals over the red carpet in church. A blonde, sour-faced creature almost as tall as Timmy, she complied gracelessly with Helen's request, slouching into position with an expression of utter boredom. By contrast, the bride, whose veil was lifted off her face, smiled sweetly at the camera from a spray of honey-hued curls, clutching a large pink and white bouquet in front of her protruding stomach.

"Perfect," Helen announced, showing Rex the digital image.

"Aye, verra nice."

"Who did your hair, Polly?" she asked. "It looks lovely."

"Amber. She stayed over last night to help me get ready. And she did my makeup."

A bit heavy on the makeup, Rex thought.

"Haven't seen Gwen, have you?" Bobby Carter asked chummily, strolling toward Rex.

"Sorry. I don't know who Gwen is."

"Polly's aunt from Wales." Carter pulled a slim cigar from his waistcoat pocket. "Mabel went to pick her up from the train station this morning while Victoria was busy with preparations at the house, but Gwen wasn't there. Unlike the old girl to miss a good knees-up. She was due to get in at 9:45. Wonder where she got to …" Chewing on the cigar, he wandered back toward the twittering bridesmaids, inquiring after the missing aunt.

"Try her mobile," Mrs. Newcombe instructed.

"She doesn't have one."

"Gwendolyn is about as much use as her brother." Mrs. Newcombe's shrill voice carried far and wide. "I don't know why we invited her."

"Well, er, there isn't much family on the bride's side," Carter pointed out in a low voice, though not so low that Rex couldn't hear. "Gwen is Polly's only other surviving relative, assuming, of course, Tom is dead."

"I'd make sure of it if I only knew where he was," Victoria Newcombe retorted. "But he disappeared off the face of the earth, leaving me with that white elephant on the hill."

"Newcombe Court is a very fine residence, Vicky, and you are lucky to have it."

"It's the least I deserve after he abandoned me and Polly the way he did. And please don't call me 'Vicky.' It makes me feel like I should be working at Woolworth's or whatever it is now. I just worry he'll come back and claim the property after all this time."

"Now, now, Victoria. He must be dead. Any self-respecting father who saw an announcement of his daughter's engagement in *The Times* would get in contact, if only to offer his congratulations. Now, don't get yourself all riled up. Today is a special occasion and you don't want to spoil it. You have worked very hard."

"Don't I know it!"

The couple moved out of Rex's earshot, and Mrs. Newcombe went to give the photographer and videographer the benefit of her advice, pointing and gesticulating like a movie director. Helen approached, putting her camera away in her handbag.

"I got a few nice shots of the church," she told Rex. "All Saints' is beautiful, isn't it?"

Rex thought it looked rather sinister beneath the dark clouds that threatened more rain. "Leave room on your camera for the 'white elephant on the hill,'" he murmured.

Helen darted at him a look of surprise. "Where did you hear that? You must mean Newcombe Court."

"Mrs. Newcombe referred to it that way, and now I'm most curious to see it for myself."

"Victoria was always complaining about its upkeep, but it makes her feel very lady of the manor."

"I can only pity poor Timmy—an overly protective mother on the one side and an overbearing mother-in-law on the other."

"Victoria's all right once you get to know her, I suppose. She's had such a lot to deal with, but today is her crowning success, marrying her daughter to a respectable accountant. I'm looking at things from her point of view," Helen added quickly, noting Rex's raised eyebrow.

"Victoria Newcombe certainly is the epitome of pretentiousness," he agreed.

"Just wait until you see Newcombe Court."

"You said that before. I cannot wait to see the blasted place. And I'm dying for a beer."

"Oh, they won't be serving beer. Far too common," Helen said in a mock-superior tone.

In that case…, Rex thought slyly. He told Helen he would bring the car round.

"Can we cadge a lift off you, if you're going to the reception?" asked a tawny-haired girl. A cream cashmere sweater overlaid with a string of pearls showed beneath her coat, a woolen beret stuffed in the pocket. "I'm Meredith, an old school friend of Polly's. And this is my boyfriend Reggie. We got the train up from London and took a taxi to Aston so we're without transport. Hello, Miss d'Arcy."

"You can call me Helen now," Rex's fiancée said with a smile. "And of course you can ride with us. How are you? It's been a while since I last saw you."

"Fine, thanks, Helen. I heard about the engagement. Congratulations." The girl's soft brown eyes took in Rex with a curious and kindly glance. A nice, wholesome lass, he decided. A little long in the face and nose, but with beautiful level brows and an upper lip shaped like a Cupid's bow. So much more appealing than the bridal troupe in their pink frills and fussy ribbons. He turned to the boyfriend and extended his hand.

"How's it going," Reggie said in a transatlantic accent that Rex thought might be an affectation; difficult to tell these days with young people adopting American slang and expressions. And turning up to a wedding in a suede jacket and jeans! Though Reggie *had* managed to throw on a tie—a mangy sherbet yellow one that looked as though it had been rescued from a thrift shop.

Rex attributed his testy mood to an overdue beer, or perhaps to the fact he was trying to quit pipe-smoking. Right now a quick trip to the pub would restore his spirits, but his ploy of offering to bring the car round so he could sneak in a drink looked as though it might be sabotaged by Meredith and Reggie, who stood on either side of him in the manner of two newly adopted puppies. Still, they were of legal age … "Fancy a quick one at the pub?" he asked. "While we wait for the wedding party to set off?"

Reggie's boyish face broke into an approving grin, but Helen quickly vetoed the idea. "I think they're getting ready to leave, and I'm not sure I'd remember the way to Newcombe if we got left behind."

Rex demurred from pointing out that if Newcombe Court was the monstrous Folly she had described, all they need do was ask its whereabouts from one of the locals.

At that moment, a rotund woman swathed in purple chiffon bounced out of a black taxi cab. "Did I miss anything?" she cried to nobody in particular.

"Just the wedding ceremony," Rex told her with a straight face.

The latecomer was in her early fifties, her black hair parted center and smoothed back in a sleek bun. Dark eyes twinkled as

23

she gazed up at him with flushed cheeks. "The train from Cardiff was late. Got here as quick as I could. Oh, dear."

"The newlyweds probably didn't even notice your absence in all the excitement," he consoled her.

"Oh, but I'm Aunt Gwen. Polly's father was my brother. I say 'was' as I haven't heard from him in ten years. He may be dead for all I know. Or else living abroad. He always did like to travel. Oh, dear," she repeated. "Still, Church of England and Church of Wales weddings are all much the same, aren't they? But you're from Scotland, I can tell from your accent. Are you here by yourself? On the bride's side or the groom's?"

"I'm with my fiancée," Rex answered, amused by the sing-song deluge of words. "We're here for the bride."

Aunt Gwen looked positively deflated when he mentioned the word *fiancée.* "Oh, just my luck. You are a very attractive man, but no doubt there will be some single gentlemen at the reception. Ta-ra for now." Fluttering a wave in his direction, she twirled away on feet incongruously dainty for a woman of her round proportions.

Reggie whooped with glee. "Helen," he said, interrupting her conversation with Meredith. "That Welsh chick just tried to pick up your man."

"It happens all the time," Helen replied with a mischievous wink. "Must be the red hair and whiskers. Or maybe the gruff Scots burr."

"I think the fact that I'm big and brawny may have something to do with it."

"That too."

Just then, the crowd behind them stirred and they watched as the newlyweds made a dash beneath a snowfall of confetti to a waiting satin pink Mercedes, whose hood ornament anchored a white ribbon forming a V across the bonnet. At the last moment, Polly whirled her bouquet into the crowd where it landed in Aunt Gwen's outstretched hands, much to the joyful surprise of the recipient.

The Mercedes pulled sedately away from the lychgate revealing to the onlookers the words *Just married* sprayed in curly white letters across the tinted rear window.

"Time we were going," Helen said when people started moving toward their cars. "You don't mind squeezing into the back?" she asked Meredith and Reggie, leading them to her Renault.

Reggie let his girlfriend in first. When they were all installed, Helen eased the car out of its space and slipped in among the row of cars making its way to the reception.

"Did you like the wedding ceremony?" she asked her young passengers, glancing into the rearview mirror.

"Thought it dragged on a bit, to be honest," Reggie said. "I don't know if I'd want something so formal for my wedding."

"I thought it was romantic," his girlfriend countered. "It should be formal. It's, like, the most important day of your life."

"For a girl," Reggie scoffed, and received a punch in the arm from Meredith. "I thought Timmy was going to bolt. He looked dead nervous."

"Well, it's a big day, like Meredith said," Helen remarked as she slowly navigated the car down the high street, stopping briefly to let the Littons' vehicle squeeze in ahead of them.

"Timmy's been having stomach problems," Meredith explained. "Polly phoned me last week to say they were thinking of postponing the wedding. But, of course, all the arrangements had been made and the invitations sent out. Then I got a call from her saying Timmy was feeling better."

"Thought we'd never make it anyway," Reggie said. "We were stuck on the stupid train about twenty minutes from Derby."

"Don't tell me," Rex said. "Mechanical problems."

"Actually, there was a body on the tracks."

"You're joking!" Helen said.

"Swear to God," Reggie told her. "Somebody jumped off the bridge. We had to wait for ages while the police investigated and the person was finally carted away in a mortuary van."

"Some passengers got off to watch," Meredith added. "It seemed a bit ghoulish, so we stayed in our compartment, but people were discussing it up and down the train."

"How awful. Was it a young person?" Helen asked. "That always seems worse."

"Don't know," Reggie replied. "Someone said the body was so badly mangled from an oncoming train it was hard to tell."

"Oh, goodness," Helen said. "I shouldn't have asked. What a terrible thing to talk about at a wedding."

As drizzle began to trickle down the car windows, she set the wipers in motion. At the White Hart Inn, the pink Mercedes turned onto Weston Road and led the slow line of cars into the gently un-dulating South Derbyshire countryside.

Rex thought it felt more like a funeral procession.

QUO VADIS
———

THE CORTEGE CLIMBED A long incline past meadows brimming with cowslip and fields where soggy sheep grazed in the lush grass. The line of cars slowed to a crawl as it passed through a pair of tall iron gates and followed along a semicircular driveway bisecting the grass parkland. Standing sentry at regular intervals, life-size white statues of graceful limbed women draped in stolas gazed blindly from blank stone eyes at the procession. Two men in anoraks directed the vehicles to parking spaces at the apex of the gravel driveway.

"You've got to be joking," Reggie said before Rex had time to formulate his own astonishment at the structure looming before him, the central part of which comprised a red brick fort six stories high, each level punctured by a lancet window set directly above the front door, culminating in a gray crenellated parapet, reminiscent of All Saints' Church in Aston.

Flanking the narrow fort, symmetrical extensions presented a lower wall of stone and a projecting upper story of white plaster façade interlaced with black timber and inset with recessed diamond pane windows. What should, thematically, have been a thatch roof instead continued the turret design of the tower. Climbing rose, clematis, and white honeysuckle lent a certain cottage charm, but failed to soften the austere aspect of the central fort whose brick wall rose to three times the height of the mock Tudor wings.

The pink Mercedes pulled up in front of an iron-studded oak door, pierced with a portcullis window. The door opened to reveal a woman in a white blouse, black skirt, and low heels, who stood aside as the wedding party mounted the shallow flight of steps draped in rain-saturated red carpet.

"It can't decide whether it wants to be a fortress or a manor house," Rex said, examining the building with curiosity through the windshield while Helen parked the car behind a white van.

"I know," Meredith said with a sigh. "It's hideous. I used to stay here weekends and pretend I was on a set for the shooting of a film about Henry VIII."

"What is its history?" Rex asked.

"The fort was built in the mid 1800s by Mrs. Newcombe's husband's great-great-grandfather or something. The wall surrounding the four acres of property was Mr. Newcombe's grandfather's doing after he sold off some of the land, and he converted the carriage house into a garage. The wings were added in the 1980s by Mr. Newcombe's parents, who passed away before he married Victoria."

"What happened to Mr. Newcombe?" Rex asked Meredith, recalling the conversation between Bobby Carter and Mrs. Newcombe.

"Nobody knows."

The four occupants of the Renault got out and made their way to the front steps of the fort. A date-stone embedded in the brickwork above the door was inscribed with *1855* and two Latin words: *Quo Vadis,* which Rex translated poetically as "Whither goest thou?" for the benefit of his companions. He explained that Latin had no interrogation point, the question being implied in the "quo."

"Is it a motto?" Meredith's boyfriend asked.

"I suppose it could be a philosophical one. Do you know where you're going in life, Reggie?"

"Haven't a clue. What about you?"

"It's taken me long enough to get where I am."

"Where's that then?"

"Queen's Counsel at the High Court of Justiciary in Edinburgh."

"Sounds impressive," Reggie said with a respectful nod. "So's this place in a fakey sort of way."

Red carpet squelched underfoot as they mounted the steps. The woman at the door took Meredith's coat and beret. Rex made sure to dry his shoes carefully on the mat before entering the great hall, which extended the breadth of the fort.

A massive stone fireplace at either side created an illusion of warmth and welcome, mitigating the starkness of the brick walls that cried out for gleaming suits of armor and a pair of crossed halberds to complete the effect of a medieval castle. Instead, tapestries of pastoral scenes, looking suspiciously like replicas to Rex's critical eye, adorned the four soaring walls, while floral rugs, on which gathered tight knots of people, covered the flagstone floor.

The guests had not yet availed themselves of the groupings of faux antique sofas, as they waited for the rest of the invitees to arrive. Amber, the sourpuss maid of honor, chatted with Polly, but her eyes were fixed on Dudley Thorpe as on an irresistible pair of shoes she could never afford. Rex sensed drama afoot.

In the back right-hand corner of the hall, a cylindrical tower built of curved blocks of stone signaled a spiral stairway. A centered archway led into its murky depths, gaping dark and sinister as a grotto and secretive as a shell. Rex fancifully imagined a dungeon lurking beneath the flagstone floor, with rusty implements of torture attached to dank walls impregnated with ghostly cries.

In the opposite corner, a DJ station stood empty, two mammoth speakers facing into the hall. A girl in a short black dress, black stockings, and white apron, offered guests flutes of champagne from a silver tray. Reggie and Meredith took theirs and eagerly went off to explore.

"Don't mind if I do," Rex thanked the server, whisking a glass off the tray and clinking it with Helen's. "No doubt there'll be plenty of toasts later on, but, for now, *Slàinte.*" He downed half the contents. "That's better," he said. "Though a beer would have done just as well."

"The bar and buffet are through here," announced the woman who had opened the front door to them, making Rex wonder whether she had overheard his comment.

He followed into an adjoining room. Spacious, yet with a low beamed ceiling, the reception area was decked out in silky chintz fabric and rococo furniture. A tri-panel Chinese lacquer screen, depicting stylized peacocks, stood in front of the far door to deter guests from venturing beyond that point. Pink and white floral arrangements graced the marble-top tables, while soft romantic hits played in the background. Against the French doors across the salon, a long table draped in white linen held the wedding gifts. Remembering the box under his arm, Rex added the fruit bowl to the collection.

To his relief, he was able to procure a pint of Guinness from the full-service bar.

"I never saw anyone so indecently pregnant!" hissed a snarky female voice. "Isn't Polly a bit far along to be flying to Majorca for her honeymoon?"

Rex pretended not to hear. "Shotgun wedding" was the next indignant phrase to assail his ears. He was about to turn and upbraid the gossipers with a sharp look of rebuke when an authoritative voice interrupted him.

"Helen!" Victoria Newcombe air-kissed his fiancée on the cheek. "Thank you so much for coming."

Mrs. Newcombe had removed her hat, and Rex found she stood up commendably to close scrutiny. A blonder and slimmer version of her daughter, her flawless makeup accentuated well-modeled bones, her body, as youthful as her face, evidently no stranger to a regular workout routine. "Sorry I didn't get around to greeting you at the church," she told them both, "but I was so busy. Honestly, once I'm through with this, I won't know what to do with myself!"

"You've done a wonderful job," Helen dutifully replied. "Everything is perfect. This is my fiancé, Rex Graves."

"Nice to meet you, Mr. Graves. I am so happy for Helen. Just goes to show—one should never give up! Ah, the vicar has arrived." The elderly man, divested of surplice, hesitated in the doorway.

"Catch up with you later, darling," Victoria Newcombe promised Helen as she breezed off in the clergyman's direction.

"Never give up!" Helen mimicked in good humor when their hostess was far enough away not to hear. "She's one to talk! I suspect Bobby Carter has been keeping her company in her husband's long absence."

"He's somewhat older than Victoria, isn't he?"

"Somewhat," Helen said enigmatically.

Rex wrapped an arm around her waist and watched the guests congregate at the bar. Helen's ex-boyfriend, taller and more athletic than Rex had anticipated, stood with the bride and groom. His date, glimpsed from the back in church, now faced them, clad in a slinky silver sequined dress, one hand possessively encircling Clive's arm. Hmm, Rex thought; Clive has great taste in women. "Aye, verra nice," he let slip.

"Rex, are you looking for a kick in the shins?" Helen inquired.

"I prefer blondes. And if you were a redhead, I'd prefer redheads."

"Watch it, or I'll pour this champagne all over your red head."

Clive guided his companion toward them with what Rex took to be a smile of triumph. The teacher blinked as he announced, "Helen, I'd like to present Jasmina," as though he were presenting a trophy.

The two women clasped hands, Jasmina emitting a nervous little giggle. The silver hoops on her ears offset the smooth honey matte of her skin. Adeptly applied black liquid liner underscored almond-shaped eyes of shiny licorice. By and by, Rex became aware of Helen's insistent gaze on his own face and slid his eyes to Clive's more pedestrian features. Stepping forward and introducing himself, he shook the teacher's hand. As predicted—a wimpy grip.

"Down for the weekend?" Clive asked.

"That's right. Hope to go hiking in the Peak District tomorrow."

"Helen told me you were an avid walker," Clive said, making Rex wonder what else she had told him in his regard. Her ex launched into a rapturous soliloquy about the District's rugged charm and recommended which trails to take, blinking all the while and leading Rex to suppose he was trying contact lenses, or else his current pair was drying up on him. It made Rex feel a compulsion to blink too. Soon bored by Clive's hyper enthusiasm, he listened with one ear to the women's conversation.

"I love Polly's gown," Jasmina said. "Antique lace. Must have cost a fortune."

"And your dress is simply gorgeous," Helen complimented.

"Oh, thanks." Jasmina giggled and sipped her champagne.

"Are you a designer?"

"Oh, no. I'm in media. Clothes are just a hobby." Another giggly squeal. "And you?"

"Student advisor at Clive's school." Helen glanced at her ex as though surprised he had not mentioned this fact to Jasmina.

"Oh—right," Jasmina said. "And that's how you know Polly...," she ventured.

"Yes, I got to know Polly during her teenage years. And, to some extent, Timmy. Timmy was Clive's pupil."

Jasmina gazed adoringly at Clive as though mathematics was the sexiest subject ever, and gave his arm a playful tweak. "Thanks to you, he became an accountant."

A pleased flush crept over Clive's bland face. "Oh, I don't know that I can take all the credit," he said, obviously ready to do just that.

"Funny to see them both grown up and married," Helen remarked, waggling her fingers at the newlyweds across the room. "Timmy has perked up. Probably glad to get the wedding ceremony out of the way."

"I know!" Jasmina said. "He was so nervous, he kept asking the vicar to repeat the prompts."

Rex asked Clive if he would like another beer and when Clive declined, went off to get one for himself, hoping to find an interesting guest to talk to. Preferably someone who knew something about Tom Newcombe, their hostess's conspicuously absent husband. He decided the sister, the garrulous aunt from Wales, might be a good start.

"SO GWEN TURNED UP in time to catch the bridal bouquet," Rex remarked to Bobby Carter, who was standing at the drinks table waiting for the bartender to finish serving a guest.

"Better late than never, I suppose. Mr. Graves, isn't it? What's your poison?" Carter relayed Rex's order to the bartender and requested another scotch for himself. "Have you visited Newcombe Court before?" he asked.

"No, never had the pleasure. Meredith, one of Polly's friends, was telling us a bit about its history on the drive over."

"It does have some historical interest," Carter acknowledged as they moved away from the bar with their drinks. "The National Trust would be very interested in acquiring it. They'd probably tear down the wings and restore it to its original glory. There used to be a moat and drawbridge, but the moat was filled when the wings were built. The dungeon is now used as a wine cellar. Mr. Newcombe liked his plonk. A bit too much, actually. There was also a jousting enclosure where the orchard and meadow now stand beyond the south wall. Old Cornelius Newcombe, the first owner, was something of a military buff. Victoria removed the weapons from the hall and from the stairwell to the battlements, which she prefers to call a widow's walk. It was all too masculine for her taste."

"Have you known Mrs. Newcombe long?"

"Since she and Thomas were married. I'm the family solicitor."

"Is Mr. Newcombe deceased?" Rex didn't let on that he had been privy to the conversation between Carter and Victoria outside the church.

"We don't know. That's the devil of it. Victoria could have procured a divorce in all this time, but she was afraid if he came back, she might lose Newcombe Court. Without knowing what happened to him, the legal situation regarding this property is somewhat vague, especially as he has a living sister."

"What, ehm, were the circumstances of his disappearance, if I might ask?" Aunt Gwen had not been able to elucidate on this point, telling Rex only that her brother had seemed unhappy and agitated the last time she saw him, which had been a decade ago.

"As long as you don't ask Victoria about it," the solicitor cautioned. "She gets a bit touchy. Well, it happened that Newcombe went on a business trip to Leicester and never came back. Victoria, thinking he might be seeing another woman, failed to inform the police. I expect she hoped to avoid a scandal and thought he would return under his own steam."

"Were the police ever informed?"

"Yes, but by then the trail had gone cold. People's memories had faded and no one could say for certain when or where he was last seen. He dealt in antiques and went all over the country."

"He never checked into a hotel? His car was never recovered?" Rex had covered a missing persons case in the past.

"He usually took the train from Derby to wherever he was going. Actually," and here Carter coughed discreetly, "he had a suspended licence. And no hotel reservation was made for that last trip. Ah, there's my girl," he bellowed, wrapping his arm around Polly's substantial waist. Sleepy-eyed, she rested her head on his shoulder. "Bearing up?" he asked. "Not too tired after being on your feet all morning?"

"My shoes are pinching a bit. My feet have swollen up disgustingly since the pregnancy," she added, smiling apologetically at Rex beneath a surfeit of blue eye shadow.

"I don't think I've had the chance to congratulate you in person," Rex said with a slight bow. "Thank you for the invitation."

"I positively love Helen. She helped me lots."

"Excuse us, Mr. Graves. Let's get some of this delicious buffet down you, Polly, to give you strength for your wedding night." Carter chuckled as he led the bride away.

"As if!" she said with a hearty laugh. "Soon as my head hits the pillow, I'll be out like a light."

How romantic, Rex thought.

"Oh, Uncle Bobby," he heard her exclaim as they distanced themselves. "Will it ever end? I hope he's early. My back is that sore, and this little blighter kicks for England. Just wait and see—he's going to be the next Beckham or else my name's not Polly Thorpe." She laughed in wonder. "Fancy that! I'm not Polly Newcombe no more."

"*Any* more," her mother corrected in passing. "Honestly, Polly."

Helen strolled over to Rex, glass in hand. "Enjoying yourself?" she asked.

"Enormously. I've unearthed a family mystery."

"You would. And what mystery might that be?"

"The missing Mr. Newcombe."

"That's no mystery. Everybody knows about Tom Newcombe."

"Aye, but not what happened."

"Well, I can guess," Helen said meaningfully, flicking her eyes in the direction of Victoria Newcombe, who was circulating among the guests playing the gracious hostess, clearly in her element. "And you have decided to get to the bottom of it?"

"I doubt I could succeed where the police have failed."

"Don't be so transparently modest, Rex. You've done it before."

"This happened a long time ago. Still, it makes for an intriguing social event. I shall now take extra interest in the Newcombe family, knowing this big question mark hangs over their heads."

"There's only Victoria, Polly, and the merry widow from Wales who actually constitute family," Helen reminded him. "And now Timmy—and, by extension, his brash brother and coddling mother."

Aunt Gwen, alluded to by Helen as the "merry widow," stood on the other side of the reception room in the company of the bald home economics teacher and a distinguished-looking gentleman, whom Rex had noticed on the groom's side of the aisle in church. Champagne glass in one hand and waving an hors-d'oeuvres on a cocktail stick in the other, the plump little Welsh lady looked to be having the time of her life as she alternately roared and hooted with laughter at what her companions were saying. Rex wondered if she bore any resemblance to her mysterious brother.

"I'm sure many a man has dreamt of simply disappearing and starting a new life," he said with a faraway gleam in his eye, prompting Helen to ask how much beer he'd had to drink. "One and a half pints. Take someone like Tom Newcombe," he pursued. "Born into a life of ease—or so I imagine, judging by this place that's been in his family for generations. He gets married, has a child. Maybe it was all too predictable. Perhaps he had a midlife crisis and decided he needed a change."

"You mean got a new identity and started over?"

Rex hitched his shoulders. "Why not? He could have had funds stashed away that no one knew about."

"Maybe Bobby Carter helped his client disappear so he could have access to the beautiful wife. Or perhaps he was murdered and his body hidden away where no one could find it."

Rex glanced at Helen in amusement. "You're intrigued as well, admit it."

"It certainly is food for thought," she conceded.

"It certainly is."

BAD OMEN

"TALKING OF FOOD, ARE you hungry?" Helen asked.

"Aye, now that you mention it. That's a pretty grand spread."

They joined the other guests at the buffet table, and Rex helped himself to giant prawns served on chipped ice and to an aromatic paella kept warm on a heating tray. Slices of roast beef, which melted off the carver's knife, followed onto his plate, along with flaky sausage rolls and a token amount of salad. Helen partook more liberally of the salad and of a slice of asparagus quiche.

"Wish we could box some of this up and take it for our picnic tomorrow," she said, moving away from the table and leading them to a sofa by a bay window overlooking the back garden.

"Why don't you just eat it now?"

"I couldn't. My waistband is already digging into my ribs."

"Undo the button on your skirt," Rex suggested practically. "No one will see under your jacket."

Helen regarded him with tenderness. "I can see that once we're married, I could end up getting lazy about my figure."

"Just don't end up the size of Polly. Och," he added, suddenly realizing what he had just said. "I don't mean *that*. That would be grand. Well, you know what I mean."

"I think I may have left it a bit late for *that*," Helen observed wistfully. "Still, I have my kids at the school."

The thought seemed to perk her up, even though he could not see the appeal of having to deal with a bunch of overwrought, oversexed, and excessively violent adolescents five days a week. And then he remembered he had to deal with overwrought, oversexed, and excessively violent individuals on a regular basis in court.

He rose with his empty plate. "Can I get you anything else while I go for a refill?"

"Just another napkin, thanks."

The drink and food had surpassed his expectations, and he was glad he had come. Discussing the people at the party with Helen on the drive home would be the icing on the cake, and then perhaps a light supper in front of the telly, followed by an early night in preparation for their hiking expedition the next morning. As he approached the buffet, Meredith and Reggie were heaping their plates in the company of another young couple, who had stood on the groom's side of the aisle in church.

"Did your dad make the cake, Elaine?" Meredith asked the girl, a gauche, wall-eyed waif in a floral print dress.

"No, Mrs. Newcombe got caterers in to do everything. In fact, one of the caterers used to work for my dad. I don't think she recognizes me. I was a mousy-haired thing back then and wore glasses with an eye patch for astigmatism."

41

Elaine had morphed into a dyed blonde with dark roots and nothing to obstruct her globular green eyes. "Her speciality was wedding cakes," she went on as Rex surveyed the food. "But they were too fancy for our shop."

"Funny she should fetch up here," Meredith said. "What are you doing now?"

"I'm helping my brother with his sandwich business. He takes his van round businesses in Derby and sells gourmet wraps to people at their desks."

"What about you then, Jeremy?" Reggie asked Elaine's boy-friend, a mild-mannered lad.

"I'm a bookkeeper for a firm in Derby. I studied accounting with Timmy. That's how we met."

Rex could see how Jeremy and Timmy had gravitated toward each other in business school. Two shy peas in a pod.

"Yeah? I work in finance too, in London," said Reggie.

"Nice."

Rex finished helping himself from the serving dishes. It was already slim pickings, as though a flock of locusts had descended upon the banquet table. Funerals were supposed to make people hungry, he reflected; perhaps the same was true of weddings. He returned to Helen, bringing her a fresh napkin.

"That bespectacled lad knows Timmy from college, and Meredith seems to be acquainted with the blonde in the flowery frock. They all seem like nice young people. Except for Dudley."

"Dudley always did stand out from the crowd."

He did so now, sounding forth to Victoria Newcombe. Rex heard the words "hot tub" and something about adding value to the home. Mrs. Newcombe answered, "We'll see" and hastily disappeared among the other guests.

When Rex had finished eating, he asked the waitress for directions to the Gents. In the great hall, he almost ran into two men moving a sofa, one the waistcoated bartender. The other wore a sleeveless black T-shirt with "DJ Smoothie" emblazoned in fluorescent green letters across the front. Bobby Carter, swaying drunkenly on the improvised dance floor, sang along to the seventies smash "If You Leave Me Now" by Chicago, while patterns of neon-colored light rippled around the lofty brick walls.

"Save a dance for me later," he called out to Polly as she swept through the reception room doorway in her long gown.

She blew him a kiss. "I will, Uncle Bobby."

"And me," Dudley said, flashing a swashbuckling smile from where he stood with the younger contingent just inside the door. Polly glared back at him and, hitching her hem up above her bare feet, flounced past Rex in the direction of the second wing, his own destination.

He continued down a corridor. Uneven white walls, designed to give this side of the house a rustic look, led to the bathroom, where he was grateful to relieve himself of a few pints of Guinness. On his way back, he saw Jasmina coming down the carpeted stairs, a wrapped box in her arms.

"Can I help you with that?" he offered.

Her almond eyes widened at the sight of him. "That's okay. It's actually quite light. I put it upstairs for safekeeping, then decided I should really put it with the other gifts, in case Polly and Timmy start opening their presents."

"Helen chose our gift. I hope they like it. I'm afraid it's not that original."

"Neither is mine." The dusky beauty let out a jangle of giggles.

"Having fun?" he asked pleasantly.

"Oh, yes. And you?"

"More than I thought I would. You know how it is when you're invited to a formal do where you don't know anybody."

"I don't know anybody either, except Clive. I hope Helen doesn't mind that I'm seeing him."

"Och, it was awhile ago when they were going out," he said, accompanying the young woman back to the party. And I don't think Clive was that great of a loss, he added privately; although Clive must have *something* to attract two lovely women like Helen and Jasmina.

He watched the apparition in the silver dress sashay through the crowd. She deposited the gift box on a nearby table. Clive beamed when he saw her and looped an arm around her slender waist.

Dudley had his eye on her too. "Not bad, is she?" he said to Rex, waving his champagne glass toward Jasmina. "Looks a bit like Pocahontas in the Disney cartoon. Right tasty. Well, they all look like models before you wed them. Then one or two kids later, they let themselves go."

Rex did not appreciate this man-to-man banter, but Dudley was the groom's twin and best man, and a measure of politeness was required, hard as it was to summon forth.

"I mean, look at Polly," the young man pursued. "She'll never get the weight off once she has the baby. That sort of weight just sticks."

"Wonder what we'd look like if we had to bear children," Rex pointed out.

"Wouldn't be so soft in the head as to get in that predicament, would we? Left to us, men wouldn't bother with that part, unless we were on the brink of extinction. My two boys are home with the flu. Last week it was earache. There's always something going on with them. Luckily there's a good doctors' practice in Aston."

"Timmy was a sickly child too, from what I understand."

"He did it for our mum's attention, me being the favourite. Psychosomatic, that's what they call it." Dudley tapped his temple. "All in the mind."

"So you live in Aston?" Rex asked, directing the conversation onto more neutral ground.

"My dad was a doctor at the surgery there. Dr. Thorpe," Dudley said with smug pride. "But he got cancer. A bit daft, if you think about it, a doctor unable to cure himself."

"I take it you didn't follow in your father's footsteps?" What a travesty that would be, Rex thought. Dudley Thorpe was about as caring and compassionate as a Komodo dragon.

"Me? Hardly. Timmy went on to college, but I couldn't take the classroom environment. I sell Jacuzzis. Good money in it and I get to travel all over the Midlands. You in the market for a hot tub?"

"Don't think so." He had never considered one for his retreat in the Highlands. Then again, a candlelit soak with Helen after a long hike in the hills might be nice...

"If you change your mind, here's my card." The stationery designated Dudley C. Thorpe as Sales Associate for Blissful Baths in Derby.

"Aye, thanks."

45

At that moment, amid a chorus of oohs and ahs, a caterer wheeled in the wedding cake, a three-tiered, heart-shaped confection topped with bride and groom miniatures. Loops of pink icing edged each white heart and, in elegant cursive across the smallest heart at the top, congratulated the happy pair by name.

"How adorable," gasped a middle-aged female guest in a sage green poplin suit, who distinctly resembled the maid of honor. "And how lethally calorific!"

"Positively yummy," Meredith said.

"The caterers outdid themselves," Victoria Newcombe crowed.

"It looks almost too good to eat." The groom's mother drilled greedy eyes into the cake, although, judging by her tiny frame, Rex deduced Mabel Thorpe ate like a bird.

He watched as she and Victoria snapped photos of the pink and white edifice. The professional photographer and videographer had not surfaced since the church ceremony, he noted; possibly to spare expense. In the picture-taking process, the cart got jostled.

"Oops, the bride has toppled flat on her face," Reggie chortled.

"Hope that's not a bad omen," someone uttered, loud enough for Rex to hear.

He had the feeling it just might be.

"CAKE, VICAR?"

THE CATERER RUSHED OVER and restored the plastic figure to an upright position, smoothing out the gouge in the white icing with a small spatula. "There, good as new," she announced. "Time to cut, I think."

"What's inside?" Aunt Gwen asked wistfully.

"Light sponge," Victoria Newcombe replied. "You must have some, Gwendolyn."

"I've sworn off sweets."

"But it's good luck for the newlyweds," Mabel Thorpe insisted.

Aunt Gwen held up small plump hands in the face of the cajoling and blandishments, and said she was determined to regain her girlish figure before she turned fifty. Rex suspected she had passed a half century by a few years.

Mrs. Newcombe summoned the young couple to cut the cake. Cameras clicked and beeped as, Timmy's hand on the bride's, they sliced into it. They wore matching gold bands, Timmy's long fingers culminating in anemic-looking nails. The newlyweds then exchanged forkfuls of cake among joyful applause while the bartender topped up the champagne.

"Cake, Vicar?"

"Thank you, Victoria."

Rex turned toward the maid of honor standing at his elbow. Her long neck and ungainly posture gave her the look of a stork. Moreover, the pink of the dress did not suit her sallow complexion, which was marred on chin and cheek by angry red bumps unsuccessfully concealed beneath beige makeup. He pitied the poor girl.

"You're Amber, are you not?" he asked convivially. "Helen told me you and Polly were at school together."

The girl's viper green eyes narrowed, clearly not welcoming the news that she had been the subject of discussion by a staff member of her old school. "What else did Miss d'Arcy tell you?" she asked tartly.

"Nothing, actually."

"Miss d'Arcy didn't tell you I left school at sixteen because I fell in the family way?" Amber demanded, seemingly put out that nothing more had been said on her account, after all.

"No." What a coy expression coming from one of Amber's generation, Rex marveled. Perhaps it had been her parents' euphemism, making what must have been something of a family drama sound like a passive event, as though their daughter had unaccountably found herself with a baby.

"Are your parents here?" he inquired.

"That's my dad other there." The distinguished man Rex had noticed in conversation with Aunt Gwen before the buffet. "He's Timmy's boss. My mum's the one in the green suit, talking to

48

Victoria." The tall bleached blonde in poplin with a fake tan and the same sour look as her daughter.

Rex nodded. "Your child—girl or boy?"

"Girl. Marie-Nicole. My younger sisters, the bridesmaids, are babysitting her this afternoon. Victoria only wanted grownups at the reception. I had to pay them double since neither one of them would mind Marie-Nicole without the other; the conniving little extortionists."

Rex chuckled, remembering the giggly girls holding the train in church. "Too much of an age gap for your daughter to be a play-mate to Polly's baby, I suppose." He looked in the bride's direc-tion where she sat, a glazed expression on her face, listening to her mother-in-law, the diminutive Mabel Thorpe.

Amber agreed. "And anyway, she's having a boy. No mistaking that from the ultrasound." Her pinched nose gave a sniff of supe-riority.

"Is she happy about that?" Rex caught on. "She won't be able to dress him in pink."

Amber laughed for the first time—a tinny, unpleasant sound. "I just *know* she wanted a girl," she imparted with evident satisfac-tion. "You can't dress boys up and put makeup on them, can you?"

"I should hope not," Rex said.

"And Timmy is such a wimp. I can't imagine him running around playing ball with his son. He's asthmatic, you know."

"Och, it might be the making of him."

Amber looked unconvinced. "He's such a change from Polly's last boyfriend. She used to go with a bloke from Aston who worked at a garage. Always had a flash car to drive. Big muscles, loads of tattoos—you know the type—" Rex got the picture. "Victoria was

49

beside herself, told Polly she wouldn't have her daughter going out with a grease monkey—only she called him an ape—and that no good would come of it." Amber's thin lips twitched. "What she probably meant was that she didn't want Polly ending up like me, in the family way."

"What did come of the relationship?"

"Her uncle Bobby paid him off."

"To stop seeing her?"

"And to disappear. But she kept on seeing him in secret for a while."

Before he could ask if Amber's father had known Polly's before he, too, disappeared, the bride came up and linked her friend's arm, smiling at Rex beneath heavy, blue-smudged lids. Polly was, he decided, a likeable girl, perhaps not the brightest of the bright, by all accounts, but open and friendly.

"Had to get away from Mabel," she told them. "My mum-in-law," she explained for Rex's benefit. "Means well but drives me up the wall with her fussing and list of do's and don't's for a girl 'in my condition.' As if I would do anything to harm her precious grandson. I mean, a bit of champagne on my wedding day won't hurt, will it?"

"I shouldn't think so," Rex said. "And you seem altogether very healthy."

"To tell the truth, I feel a bit peculiar all of a sudden. The champagne must have gone to my head. So, what have you two been talking about?" she asked Amber with a bright smile.

"Nothing much," the maid of honor fudged.

"I'll leave you two girls to it. Lovely reception, by the way, Polly." Rex patted her plump arm.

"Nice bloke," he heard her say to Amber as he wandered away in search of Helen.

"Bit old though," her friend replied.

Rex smiled to himself.

"And he's dead nosy—"

"Mr. Graves?" Victoria Newcombe's strident tones dissected his thoughts. "Would you care for some wedding cake?" She held a cake slicer above the intact third tier. The two uppermost hearts had gone, leaving moist crumbs and pink and white icing on the foil trays.

"Just a sliver, thank you. Helen, you not having any?"

"I'll just have a bit of yours." She took a forkful off his plate and deposited it in her mouth. "Mm, very good. So. I take it you didn't much like Clive?"

"It's not that I didn't like him," Rex fabricated. "It's just that if I had listened to any more of his painstaking lecture about all the delights of the Peak District, it would have spoilt my sense of wonder once I got there."

Helen fixed him with an expression of amusement. "He was being friendly and only wanted to give you the benefit of his experience. But I admit, he does go on a bit."

Boring—I always said so! Rex polished off the rest of his cake to the popping of champagne corks.

"Toasts! Toasts!" Uncle Bobby announced, brandishing a smoking bottle of Piper-Heidsieck Blanc de Blanc. "Where's Timmy? And where the dickens is Gwen *now*? Oh, well, as you were," he told the guests. "We'll wait for the groom, but it's a bit late for him to be getting cold feet."

The comment drew a genial laugh from the crowd who had gathered closer for the toasts. No sooner had they returned to their conversations than Polly gasped, and gasped again. Rex watched as she reached out and grabbed Carter's arm for support.

"Need some water," she slurred.

Never had Rex seen anyone look so green around the gills. Perspiration covered her face. Offering to get the water, he hurried to the bar where tea and coffee were being served. By the time he returned with the glass, Polly was doubled over clutching her stomach. He held out the water just as she collapsed in front of the guests in a pile of white lace.

REX KNEELED DOWN BESIDE Polly while Carter held her head in his lap and tried to put the glass of water to her lips, but she started retching and convulsing uncontrollably.

"Ambulance!" the solicitor cried, and asked everyone to stand back and give Polly some room.

"What can I do to help?" the vicar warbled.

"I'll take care of her." Victoria Newcombe crouched on the Berber carpet with a handful of white linen napkins and took Carter's place. She mopped her daughter's brow and mouth, unable to control the yellowish-green emissions oozing from the girl's lips. "Get everybody out of here," she shrieked. "Polly! Polly!"

Rex cleared the room and suggested to the bartender that the coffee and tea service be moved into the great hall. He opened the bay window to let in some air, since the stench of vomit proved nauseating. The vicar, succumbing to convulsions in turn, flopped into an armchair. Rex rushed to his aid and loosened his clerical collar. "Can I take you outside for some air, Reverend?"

"Just need w-water ... oh, let me be, dear boy," he said hoarsely, feebly pushing Rex away and covering his mouth with a handkerchief.

Rex glanced over to where Polly lay writhing on the floor. "Let's get her to a sofa," he suggested to her mother, who sat sideways and crumpled beside her, leaning forward on her hands.

Victoria looked up and he was appalled to see that she too had turned green. "Food poisoning," she said between gasps. "Prawns."

Helen and Diana Litton stood in the doorway, holding the guests at bay.

"Did someone call an ambulance?" Rex asked.

"Dudley," Helen told him. "The nearest emergency room is at Derby City Hospital. Mr. Carter went up the tower to look out for the ambulance. Timmy has been taken ill too. His mother is with him upstairs."

Polly moaned deliriously from the center of the room, Victoria Newcombe now prostrate on the floor beside her. Rex felt the vicar's faint pulse.

"I think he's unconscious."

"I'll help clean up," Diana Litton said. "I'm no stranger to vomit and all the rest of it. I nursed my late mother through years of incontinence. Meredith says she'll assist. She works as a nurse's aide."

"Anything to make them more comfortable," Rex acquiesced. "Though I'm at a loss what to do. I don't suppose there's a doctor in the house?" he asked without any real hope.

"We already asked if anyone had any sort of medical experience," Helen told him. "Only Meredith."

"Meredith seems like a capable, level-headed girl. Send her in."

"I've brought towels and disinfectant," the girl said.

"Good. Mrs. Litton will help you. Any ideas what caused this?"

Meredith's gaze swept over the victims. "My guess is bacteria in the food." She considered for a moment. "E. coli and salmonella would cause these types of symptoms, but not usually so quickly. I don't really know for sure, though. Sorry."

As Meredith and Diana ministered to the sick, Rex looked around the otherwise deserted room. The half-eaten cake with the two bride and groom figures lying side by side on the top tier presented a pitiful sight. What a tragic end to a wedding, he lamented. And everything had happened so fast.

As he left the room, he ran into Bobby Carter.

"Someone said Victoria has come down with food poisoning," the family solicitor said.

"So did Reverend Snood."

"I'll make sure Victoria sues Pembleton Caterers out of business. They assured us everything would be fresh and of the highest quality. They certainly charged enough. And now this." Carter looked into the room and took out his handkerchief, which he held up to his nose.

"Perhaps you can be of some comfort to Mrs. Newcombe and her daughter. I'll go and have a word with the caterers."

Carter raised his fist. "I'll have more than a word with those two incompetent crooks."

"Let me," Rex coaxed. "You'll be of more use here."

He went in search of the caterers and found them in the kitchen in the opposite wing. This room served as their base of operations, attested to by a couple of stainless steel mobile ovens, boxes of cutlery, and reserve piles of white plates. The two middle-aged women sat stiffly with the young waitress at a pine table laden with clean serving dishes, including a fruit bowl with a decorative border of cherries and pears.

"Any news?" asked the wiry-haired caterer who had wheeled in the cake. The other sat in stunned silence, staring into space and chewing on her pinky nail.

"Not good, I'm afraid. Four people are ill, including Timmy. We're waiting for the ambulance."

"I don't know what happened," the first woman said, helplessly lifting her hands and letting them fall back in her lap. "We've been going through the menu and can only think that the seafood might have been off. But I picked it up myself this morning from the fishmonger we always use. It was packed in ice on the way here and put straight into the refrigerator."

"The prawns smelt perfectly fresh," agreed the other caterer, whose smooth gray hair was worn in a short ponytail tied back with a black velvet ribbon. "And so did the shrimp. We inspect every item before purchase. The lettuce was thoroughly washed, and ... well, we'll be ruined, that's all there is to it."

"How long have you had the business?" Rex asked.

"Five years," her partner replied. "We're sisters. Stella and Lydia Pembleton. Rachel here is Lydia's daughter. She helps out at weekends."

"Well, let's not jump to any hasty conclusions. I just came to see if you might have thought of anything that could help explain the onset of symptoms."

"What could it be but an unfortunate case of food poisoning?" Stella Pembleton asked. "Wait. You think it was deliberate poisoning? I can only hope," she said with a grim smile. "Foul play would exonerate us."

"Even in the unlikely event it was deliberate, Pembleton Caterers would be finished," her sister Lydia countered. "No one would hire us for another event."

Rachel ran fingers through chin-length, crimped black hair, held to one side by a tortoiseshell clasp. "Imagine something like this happening on your wedding day! Poor them. What a catastrophe."

"Do you know Polly?" Rex asked the girl, who was about the same age as the bride.

"No, I just came in today to help serve and clear up."

"How did you get the catering assignment for the wedding?" he asked Stella, who appeared to be the one in charge.

"We advertise online and through leaflets we distribute to bridal shops. We prepare everything fresh and serve it on our own crockery. We provide the glasses too. We're a one-stop service and offer flowers and entertainment, and even the invitations, through Patel's Print & Post in Derby."

Rex heard a siren outside, followed by a commotion in the hall. He glanced at his watch. A good twenty minutes had passed since Polly's collapse. "No doubt we'll find out more shortly," he said. With that, he left the morose trio in the kitchen and joined the bulk of the guests by the front door.

Two green-clad paramedics entered the hall with a stretcher and, directed by the solicitor, disappeared into the living room.

"Has anyone else been taken ill?" he asked Roger Litton, whose red polka-dot bow tie added to the surreal montage of the proceedings.

"Not so far. Diana told me the vicar hasn't come round yet. I teach Home Ec, you know. Food left out on a buffet table is prone to contamination. I'm thinking the lad who was carving the roast beef might not have kept his hands scrupulously clean."

"He was wearing white gloves."

"Was he? I never noticed that. In that case, it was most likely the curried prawns."

"That does seem to be the consensus," Rex told him.

"Rex!" Helen grabbed his arm. "Where were you?"

"Talking to the caterers. This outbreak isn't good news for them." Especially if anyone died.

Rex fervently prayed that would not be the case. He'd had the feeling since looking out Helen's window that morning something might go wrong on the young couple's wedding day. How wrong, he had yet to determine.

WITCH'S BREW

"WITCH ... POTIONS," POLLY MUMBLED as, tightly wrapped in a blanket, medics propelled her to the waiting ambulance on a clattering gurney. "Witch, potions ...," her voice trailed off indistinctly.

"I suppose that is another theory," Roger Litton, the home economics teacher, remarked. "Though highly unlikely. Poor girl, but she'll be all right once they get her to the hospital. They can pump out her stomach or whatever it is they do."

"What's she going on about witches for?" Reggie asked. "This whole thing is creeping me out."

"She's delirious," Meredith told her boyfriend. "Hasn't a clue what she's saying."

"Imagine coming down poorly like that on your wedding day," Mabel said, wringing her hands and watching as Polly was lifted into the bay of the ambulance beneath the flickering red wash of lights. "Fortunately, Timmy seems to be all right now."

Uncle Bobby followed the second gurney carrying Victoria. "Can I go with you?" he asked a medic.

"No room, mate. Got to fit the vicar in. You can follow in your car if you like."

Rex watched while the medics went briskly about their business. When all three patients were loaded into the ambulance, he caught up with the crew as they were getting ready to leave and asked what might have caused such a violent reaction.

"Nausea, vomiting, and upset stomach," said one. "Best guess—acute case of food poisoning. Maybe some iffy mayonnaise. Did it come on fast?"

"Within an hour and a half or so of the buffet being served. Can you test for arsenic?"

"Arsenic? Got proof?"

"I prosecuted a case of homicidal poisoning involving arsenic once. Exact same symptoms. Just a thought…"

"Hear that, Fred?" the medic addressed his colleague. "I'll inform ER," he told Rex.

The driver slammed shut the back doors of the ambulance, muttering "bloody lawyers."

"Mr. Carter," Rex said. "I think we should gather everyone together at the first opportunity and see if we can pinpoint the source of the poisoning. Time may be of the essence."

"I heard you mention arsenic." The shock of events seemed to have sobered the solicitor up considerably.

"I think we should keep that under wraps for now so as to avoid more panic. We need to remind everyone not to touch or ingest anything."

"I was on my way to the hospital."

"I know, but I'm only a guest here, and a second-hand guest at that. You are the logical person to represent the Newcombes. Perhaps best if you stay."

"Why do you suspect intentional poisoning?"

"For one thing, the caterers don't strike me as careless. For another, Timmy Thorpe presents signs of long-term arsenic poisoning, if I'm not mistaken."

"Don't know about that," Carter said doubtfully. "He has been ill, but we all thought it was a stomach bug."

"Maybe that's what you were supposed to think. His nails tell a different story."

"His nails?" Carter all but scoffed.

"Faint white striations, called Mee's Lines. At first I thought it was due to anemia."

The solicitor blew out a heavy sigh. "If you want to try your hand at unmasking the culprit, it's your funeral. But I don't know that I want to go barging into an investigation without sufficient evidence. Lord knows, the family has been through enough."

"I appreciate your position, but we shan't be barging, merely tiptoeing. Until I can validate or refute my suspicions."

"Oh, very well, but when the police arrive, I'll go to Victoria. I take it the police have been alerted?"

"I called just before Polly was taken out to the ambulance."

"Your fiancée told me you were something of a private detective. Of murders."

"Just a hobby. A morbid hobby, granted. I'm a barrister by profession. An advocate as we call ourselves in Scotland."

"Good reasoning skills and a flair for eloquence are required for that," Carter acknowledged. "But as the Newcombe's solicitor, their interests are my first concern, which means I don't want to stir up a hornet's nest, just to play along with your hobby."

"I promise to use the utmost discretion, and your help will be invaluable."

Carter hemmed and hawed some more. "Presumably the hospital will conduct tests on the basis of your, er, supposition. At the very least, we have a case for negligence on the part of the caterers."

"And at worst, murder. Reverend Snood left here with an oxygen mask over his face. It's possible he may not survive."

"I think you may be grossly exaggerating the situation, but if what you say is true, I wouldn't mind nabbing the prankster myself and swinging him from the turrets. Could be one of the younger guests or a couple of them in cahoots. Perhaps they were practicing on Timmy."

Rex refrained from telling Carter that he thought the poisoning had been more than a prank. Too much care and thought had gone into the plan.

"Holding your own counsel on that one, eh?" Carter inquired as together they walked back across the gravel toward the front entrance of Newcombe Court. "Well, we'll see."

"*Quo Vadis*," questioned the enigmatic motto above the threshold. "Where angels fear to tread," Rex murmured in response. He felt a sudden tightening of the stomach, a cold dread in his heart. He might be wrong in his assumptions. How much Guinness and champagne had he consumed? And yet he felt in full command of his mental faculties. On reflection, it had been two beers and not much champagne.

All the same, he decided not to mention his suspicions to Helen, who would likely agree with Carter that he was seeking evil intentions where none existed.

He popped his head through the door to the vacated reception room, preparing to seal it off until the police could investigate. His gaze swept the discarded wedding veil, which lay bunched up on the floor. The cake tray, a forlorn monument to the nuptials, stood on the cart, bereft of its miniature figures. Rex did a double-take. He could have sworn they had been lying on the empty top tier when he left to talk to the caterers. They were nowhere to be seen.

Now, more than ever, he was convinced evil was indeed at work. But who was the evil-doer?

QUOD ERAT
DEMONSTRANDUM

BOBBY CARTER CONVENED THE guests, caterers, and staff in the great hall. Mrs. Thorpe led Timmy to a sofa, while Clive wrapped his arms protectively around Jasmina. Dudley had removed his jacket and stood posturing, tie loosened and brawny arms folded across his gray satin waistcoat. The DJ, clearly confused by the turn of events, turned down his music even lower.

Carter proceeded to tell everyone that the police had been notified of the outbreak and warned them against consuming anything except for sealed containers of drink. No one was to be unduly alarmed, he assured his listeners. The symptoms of the three victims who had succumbed to food poisoning were undoubtedly treatable. He trailed off by saying he hoped there would be no further occurrences.

"So the cops are coming to investigate food poisoning?" Reggie asked. "Someone said something about arsenic."

"Arsenic is naturally occurring in shellfish," Rex interjected truthfully but disingenuously before anyone could react. He did not add that arsenic in its organic form would likely not occur in dangerous doses at one sitting. "But whatever it was, the symptoms are severe. It might behoove us in the meantime to see if we can isolate the source of contamination. I, for instance, had a second helping of prawns without any ill effects—so far."

Most of the fourteen guests in the hall had partaken of the prawns, it transpired. All had eaten the roast beef with the exception of Jeremy, who was a vegetarian. Everyone present, between them, had eaten everything. An informal survey conducted on the drinks resulted in the same findings. No one acted guilty to Rex's alert eye, although many of those present appeared understandably nervous. Few at most could have imagined that the wedding reception would end in disaster.

"Polly mentioned something about potions when she was being wheeled out to the ambulance," Reggie recalled. "She drank champagne."

"Respectful of her condition, Polly drank only a small amount of champagne," Rex elaborated. This had been served to the guests upon arrival, randomly. The bottles served at the toasting had been popped open in front of everyone, which precluded anyone from spiking them. "It appears everyone had champagne," he concluded. "Does anybody have any other ideas?"

"Could Victoria, Polly, and the vicar have consumed anything different?" Tom Willington, Timmy's boss at the accounting firm, asked Stella Pembleton. A tall, handsome man in his mid forties with silver-threaded sideburns, he was dressed in an impeccable pinstripe suit that could have been tailor made for his athletic physique.

The caterer shook her head resolutely, setting in motion her short gray frizz. "Not unless Mrs. Newcombe offered them something from the family kitchen in the other wing. And I don't know why she would. Everyone started with a glass of champagne and cheese hors-d'oeuvres. Then it was on to the buffet and cake."

The cake, Rex mused. Victoria, Polly, and the vicar had eaten the cake, as had Timmy, who was also taken ill. "Who had cake from the top tier?" he asked.

Mrs. Thorpe raised her hand. "I did," she said, clasping at the fake pearls at her throat.

"If you are feeling okay, don't worry unduly."

"I have been feeling a bit wobbly, but my first concern was for Timmy. We're both fine now."

"Dudley, did you have cake?" Rex asked.

"Not me."

"Mr. Carter?"

"I didn't touch it, as it so happens. Are you suggesting…?"

Rex pensively raised a finger, forestalling the question while he pursued his train of thought. "And Aunt Gwen said something about having sworn off sweets in anticipation of her fiftieth birthday. Who else was served from the top tier?" he asked the guests.

No hands went up. Amber, the maid of honor, said she received the first slice from the second tier, followed by her parents. "The top heart was all gone," she explained.

"I had seconds," Reggie told Rex. "Jeremy did too, didn't you, mate? We were served from the bottom tier."

"There was loads left," Jeremy said apologetically.

66

"Ms. Pembleton, did you have some cake?" Rex inquired.

"Yes. So did Lydia and Rachel. After everyone was served, Mrs. Newcombe offered the staff and DJ a slice."

Rex turned to Bobby Carter. "*Quod erat demonstrandum.*"

"The top layer of cake, hmm? You may have something there."

Especially since the miniature bride and groom seem to have vanished, Rex thought. "Where is Aunt Gwen?" he asked Carter.

Nonplussed, Carter shrugged his shoulders. "Haven't seen her since... I don't rightly recall, but I think it was at the cake-cutting. She wasn't in the tower when I went up to see where the ambulance had got to. Too wet for a stroll in the garden..." He turned to the group in the hall. "Mrs. Gwendolyn Jones from Wales. Short, plumpish woman in a mauve dress. Anyone seen her?"

Nobody had, and the solicitor took off to look for her.

"What do we do now?" a shrill voice demanded from the crowd.

Rex saw the voice belonged to Amber's mother, the shrewish blonde in the sage green suit. "I suggest we make ourselves as comfortable as possible while we wait for the police."

"I don't want to wait," the woman objected. "Why can't we leave our names and phone numbers? The police can then contact us at their leisure."

Murmurs of agreement arose from the guests.

"I don't think the police will be treating the poisoning in a leisurely manner, Mrs...?"

"Jocelyn Willington. My husband is Timmy Thorpe's boss."

"So we're saying someone deliberately poisoned the cake?" DJ Smoothie spoke for the first time, sitting forward in his seat, gym-sculpted biceps bulging from black T-shirt holes as he rested his elbows on the knees of frayed jeans. "I mean, you don't usually get that sick from eating cake, not from just one slice. Usually it's chicken or eggs or summat like that." Rex noted the DJ's broad Derbyshire dialect, acutely at odds with the Elvis Presley hair.

"Nothing has been confirmed yet, but process of elimination points to the cake." And, Rex thought, the onset of symptoms occurred within half an hour of its consumption, which would be about right for acute arsenic poisoning.

The DJ tugged at his dark locks. "Just my bleeding luck. We'll be here all day and I have another gig later."

Rex turned his attention back to Mrs. Willington. "It will make their job harder if we all take off home and the police have to track us down individually. And I'm sure we all feel we owe it to our hostess, who invited us here to celebrate her daughter's wedding, to get to the bottom of this." Ms. Willington's sourly pursed lips conveyed she did not feel she owed Victoria Newcombe this huge imposition on her time, though she said nothing. "So perhaps we could confine ourselves to the hall and continue to keep calm," he suggested.

Any possibility of calm was shattered when Bobby Carter burst into the hall from the door to the caterers' wing. "Mr. Graves," he declared. "We need to get the police here at once! Victoria's collection of antique snuff boxes has gone missing from the upstairs study and Aunt Gwen is nowhere to be found in the house."

What else could possibly go wrong at a wedding, Rex wondered?

REX WASN'T TOO CONCERNED about missing snuff boxes at this point. However, upon reflection, it might conceivably shed light on the poisoning. He asked Carter to explain about the alleged theft, and was informed that an assortment of valuable Georgian and early Victorian snuff boxes, many of them exquisite and in some cases unique, had simply vanished.

"Gentlemen in the nineteenth century were fond of snuffing tobacco after dinner with their port and brandy, and liked to show off their boxes," the solicitor recounted. "Cornelius Newcombe, the founder of Newcombe Court, started the collection. It was added to by Thomas Newcombe. What a damned thing to have happen when poor Victoria and her daughter are laid up in hospital! Perhaps I should try calling again."

Just then Rex heard the crunch of tires on gravel outside on the driveway. Stella Pembleton opened the door to admit a young constable, who took off his hat and hesitated in front of the expectant gathering.

"Are you by yourself?" Carter demanded, peering around the policeman.

"Just until reinforcements arrive," the copper answered gamely, extracting a notepad and pencil from the breast pocket of his uniform. He was a fresh-faced lump of a lad, and Rex thought at first someone might be playing a practical joke, especially when he introduced himself as PC Dimley. In addition, he spoke with braying Midland vowels that made him sound like a yokel. "So what have we here?" he asked.

"We now have a theft of family heirlooms on top of a case of poisoning of some description," Carter informed him. "The snuff boxes were here this morning. We need a detective."

"All in good time. Are you Mr. Newcombe?"

"No, I am not, but I feel responsible. I am the Newcombes' solicitor. The lady of the house is in hospital, along with her daughter and Reverend Snood of All Saints' Church in Aston. They were taken ill at the wedding reception. Besides which, we have a missing guest—one Gwendolyn Jones—who arrived from Wales this morning." Carter was practically hyperventilating by now, the quills on his scalp all a-quiver.

"Quite a lot going on then, sir," PC Dimley agreed, scribbling away on his pad. "Anything else?"

"Isn't that enough?"

"I would say so, sir. If I could just have your name."

Bobby Carter provided him with that information.

"And this gentleman next to you?" the constable inquired.

"Reginald Graves, QC," Rex answered. "I came as a wedding guest with my fiancée, Helen d'Arcy, from Derby."

"Thank you, sir. If we could continue around the room so I can get everyone's name, home address, and car registration..."

Jocelyn Willington let out an exasperated sigh. "How long is this going to take, Constable?"

"It might be awhile, ma'am. Why don't you all take a seat?"

The younger guests gravitated toward the massive fireplace on the right and settled around the broad stone lintel propped up by a pair of spiral columns. The older generation gathered around the hearth across the hall. The catering staff huddled farther back, near where the DJ's equipment stood silent.

While the constable was busy with the staff from Helen's school, Rex pulled Bobby Carter aside. "How much would the entire collection of snuff boxes fetch?" he asked.

"It's insured for half a million pounds. There are forty snuff boxes in all. A gold case similar to one in Victoria's collection, dating back to the 1830s, went to auction at Bonhams in Knightsbridge for forty thousand pounds. When opened, it displayed a rather saucy scene of two couples misbehaving in a garden." Carter helped himself to a cup of coffee from a large urn on the refreshment table. "It's uncontaminated," he assured Rex. "I watched the man open a new tin of Maxwell House and use water from a sealed bottle." He took a sip and nodded. "Tastes all right."

"Forty thousand pounds," Rex mused aloud.

"Another snuff box, engraved in silver, fetched upward of thirty grand. A private investor from Holland acquired that one. Victoria owned several boxes in silver and a painted enamel one that played 'Greensleeves.' That's her favourite." Carter seemed to recollect himself and frowned. "I suppose the poisoning was planned to create a diversion while the collection was stolen from upstairs."

"Why not just sneak into the house at night or when the occupants were out?"

"Burglar system. Victoria is paranoid about break-ins. And no one would expect close friends and family to abscond with the family jewels, as it were. Dreadful business." Carter chugged down more coffee.

"Is it possible Aunt Gwen decided to take what she thought was rightfully hers? She is Tom Newcombe's sister, after all."

"She's never shown any interest in Newcombe Court or its contents. Her late husband left her quite well off. I wonder," Carter said, knitting his furry brows. "Do you think she was kidnapped?"

"By whom? An intruder would likely have been noticed carting off the antiques, let alone Aunt Gwen. If we are to dismiss her as a suspect, that leaves the other guests and the catering staff."

"The Pembleton sisters have their reputation to think of."

"Half a million pounds might compensate for the loss of their reputation," Rex pointed out. "However, arsenic would be a bit of overkill just to create a diversion. Why not just some defensible bacteria?"

"The waitress and the other people hired for the occasion would be less concerned about a scandal," Carter reasoned.

"The waitress is Lydia Pembleton's daughter. Were the snuff boxes kept under lock and key?"

"Many were on display around the living room where the buffet and bar were set up. The most expensive ones were locked in the glass cabinet in the study upstairs. But Victoria put them all in the study last night."

"I see." The thief had to have known that some of the boxes had been moved from their original place in the living room, Rex surmised. No one would risk lifting them under the noses of the owner, guests, and catering staff.

Deep in thought, he wandered across the flagstone floor to where the caterers sat awaiting their turn to be questioned by the constable. He pulled a vacant chair next to Stella Pembleton's. "I've been talking to Mr. Carter about the missing snuff box collection."

Ms. Pembleton sighed in desolation. "I can't help you any more with that than with the poisoning."

"I wanted to ask you a few things, to help speed the investigation along."

"I heard you're a private detective of sorts. Is that why you're involved?"

"I developed an interest in this family before anyone was taken ill and long before the snuff boxes disappeared."

Stella Pembleton contemplated the unadorned hands in her lap. "The family history is rather interesting," she agreed. "I realized Mrs. Newcombe's husband wasn't in the picture when I first came to Newcombe Court a few months ago to discuss preparations for the reception. It was a bit awkward because I didn't want to ask if he had passed away. I've since learned that nobody actually knows for sure what happened to him."

"Who else among your staff was at Newcombe Court when you came to discuss the reception?"

"My sister. Lydia is responsible for the flowers, so she sees what might be available in the garden and where the floral arrangements should go. She's the artistic one. I mainly deal with the food and drink and other logistics. We were here again the day before yesterday to finalize the details."

"What I'm driving at, Ms. Pembleton, is who might have visited the premises ahead of time and seen the contents of the house—most notably, the snuff boxes?"

"Only Lydia and myself. My sister did remark on one of the boxes, a musical one in enamel that was on the mantelpiece, and Mrs. Newcombe obligingly told us about the collection and, rather indiscreetly, I suppose, let slip how valuable it was. I suggested she move all the valuables from the room to avoid damage. I've seen it happen before where a drunk guest knocks over a vase or spills red wine on the carpet. Better safe than sorry, I always tell my clients."

Rex reflected that her client in this case was less than safe and no doubt more than a little sorry. "Anyone else on the outside who might have known about the snuff boxes?"

"I may have mentioned the fact to one of my team."

"Which one?"

Stella Pembleton shook her head in frustration. "I don't mean anyone in particular. I just mean that when you are putting an event together, things get said in passing. When we arrived early this morning, the valuables had been moved from the living room per my suggestion. The bartender and buffet attendant set up their stations. Lydia did the flowers while I oversaw the kitchen preparations. Rachel rolled the napkins containing the silverware. I can vouch for Rachel. She's a hard-working girl who wouldn't do anything to disgrace her mother."

"When did the DJ arrive?"

"Just before the guests. He's often late, but he's a great success at these events. If we can't get him, we use another DJ. We carefully vetted DJ Smoothie, the bartender, and the carver before we employed them. Each came highly recommended." Stella Pembleton folded her arms tightly across the front of her blouse. "I can't believe it's any of them."

At that juncture, Bobby Carter came up to Rex, his ruddy face two shades paler than when Rex had first met him. "A word in your ear, Mr. Graves," he murmured. "Bad news, I'm afraid."

"You mean, more bad news," Rex corrected him. What, he wondered, could have happened now?

REX THANKED STELLA PEMBLETON for her time and followed Carter into the cozy living room in the caterers' wing, out of earshot of the rest of the wedding party.

"PC Dimley got an update from the hospital," the solicitor said gravely. "Reverend Snood was dead on arrival. It's touch and go for Victoria. They've got her on dimercaprol and are treating her for dehydration. Polly is undergoing an emergency C-section to save the baby. That's all the constable could tell me, but it's more than I managed to get from the hospital myself."

News of the elderly vicar's death came as a sad shock to Rex, but no great surprise. "Was arsenic poisoning confirmed?"

The solicitor nodded. "The fatal stuff. Fast acting. Arsenic trioxide."

Rex nodded, troubled to have been proved right. He wondered how much of it had passed through the mother's placenta into the unborn child. "I am so very sorry." He placed a hand on Carter's shoulder. "The child won't be very premature, though."

"No, that much is fortunate. Polly was eight months along." Carter roused himself. "What do you know about arsenic trioxide?"

"That it comes in a white powder, and is odorless and tasteless, so would have been a piece of cake to put in the cake—if you'll forgive the pun."

Carter regarded him as though he might be a little mad, but stress sometimes made Rex veer into levity, and gallows humor when the occasion prompted. "Where can you get it?" the solicitor asked.

"In the case I prosecuted where a young man was accused of poisoning his grandmother, he got it from rat poison. He told the court his grandmother had rats in her attic, which turned out to be true. Unlike Grandmother, however, they were still alive and kicking."

Carter sank into a capacious armchair and stared into space.

"Can I get you anything, Mr. Carter? More coffee?"

"I'll be all right, thank you. I just need to be on my own for awhile. It's a lot to absorb."

"Right you are." After giving the solicitor a comforting squeeze on the shoulder, Rex slipped into the great hall, quietly closing the living room door behind him.

The guests appeared much the same as before, grouped around the fireplaces, chatting and whispering, but clearly growing impatient with the constable's progress. Rex deduced that news of the vicar must not have spread. Best keep it that way, if possible.

Helen met him in the center of the room. "I saw the constable take Bobby Carter aside. Is there any news?"

"The vicar never recovered consciousness, Helen. And Mrs. Newcombe is still in danger. The reports on Polly and the baby seem "more promising." This was the best interpretation he could give of the information he had received secondhand from Carter. He did not want to upset his fiancée, but even so, tears sprang to her eyes, which she swiped away.

"An innocent woman and child," she whispered fiercely.

"Helen, did you see the wedding cake before it was brought into the reception room?"

"It was in the caterers' kitchen. Polly showed it to me. Stella Pembleton was just putting the finishing touches on it—decorative hearts and rosebuds, and whatnot." Helen glanced about her and said in a low voice, "I don't think PC Dimley is up to the job. He looks so young and inexperienced. Shouldn't there be a detective on the case?"

"There will be. The important thing is that Dimley is maintaining order and doing a methodical job of talking to everyone in turn."

The constable was now addressing the younger guests—Meredith, Reggie, Jeremy, and his girlfriend in the dowdy floral dress.

"Can I drive you to the hospital?" Rex went to ask Timmy, who would have been notified of developments at the hospital by now.

The groom shook his head timorously, the angular planes of his face chalky and strained in the firelight. "My mother says Polly will be out of it and won't know I'm there, and the shock of seeing her might bring on my asthma."

"Might be an idea to get yourself checked out, all the same. You had similar symptoms yourself, didn't you, even if they were milder?"

"Mum says I'm okay. She gave me charcoal tablets. I've been having a funny tummy, that's all."

Rex wondered if Timmy always did what Mabel told him, which might not bode well for happy married life. Though natural enough she might be over-protective of a son who had been sickly as a child, that son had obligations to a wife and child of his own now.

He crouched beside the young man's chair. "When Polly comes round, it will be a comfort for her to know you're there."

Mabel appeared out of nowhere and glared down at him.

"Please don't upset Timmy. He's very susceptible to emotion." The whiskers growing out of the mole on her chin trembled distractingly. Rex focused instead on her beaky nose and accusing eyes, the same pallid blue as Timmy's and reminiscent of a dreary spring sky.

"I was offering to drive him to the hospital to see his wife and child."

"I would take him myself if I felt it was necessary. And the policeman wants us to stay until his superiors arrive."

Rex rose to his feet, towering over the woman. He doubted PC Dimley would be so callous as to disallow her son a visit to the hospital. However, it was clear from Mabel's rigid expression that her mind was made up. "Well, let me know if I can be of any assistance," he replied stiffly and, with a courteous nod at Timmy, returned to Helen.

"I just got a dressing down from Mabel Thorpe for interfering in family business," he reported.

"She's just concerned about Timmy. She used to write notes excusing him from school when he had a sniffle. Fortunately, he was a studious boy and always managed to catch up with his class work."

"Mrs. Thorpe mollycoddled him. Just look at him pitying himself when his wife and child are in danger, and Polly's mother is too sick to comfort her daughter."

Helen sighed heavily. "I know, but when Mabel lost her husband, her two sons became her whole life."

"My mother is a widow too, and I was her only son. She never let me miss a day of school. And she wouldn't tolerate any sniveling."

"I think Mabel was lonely and liked having Timmy stay home. Dudley was the exact opposite. He felt smothered. He was always the more independent of the two."

"I can't believe they're twins," Rex remarked, looking across the great hall to where Dudley draped an elbow over the carved stone lintel, chatting up Jasmina. Rex found himself wishing Clive would give him a bop on the nose, but he didn't credit Helen's ex with more spunk than timid little Timmy.

"Different eggs," Helen explained. "Timmy and Dudley don't share exactly the same DNA. That's why they aren't identical."

Jasmina's squealy giggle rang out incongruously, piercing the subdued conversations. That laugh could seriously grate on one's nerves, thought Rex, whose own nerves stood on edge, especially when Jocelyn Willington approached. She wore a funereal expression beneath her sun-bed tan and, when she placed a hand on his arm, he saw she was trembling. Her mouth worked strangely before she was finally able to speak.

"You had better come and see this before I alert the constable," she croaked through dry lips. "I doubt he's been on the force long enough to have witnessed anything like this."

"Mrs. Willington, I'm sure PC Dimley didn't join the police force so he could be protected from the world by the public he's supposed to serve. Suppose you tell me what it is you saw."

Mrs. Willington took a raspy breath and visibly steeled herself. "I just found Polly's Aunt Gwen. I still think you'd better come and see for yourself first."

"Very well. Lead the way," he said with a deep sense of foreboding.

REX HAD NOT BEEN prepared for Mrs. Willington's answer, much less the scene that awaited him. They had exited through the exterior door in the kitchen where the caterers had set up their operations, and then skirted the patio extending around the back of the fort. The bulge from the stone stairwell blocked the view on the other side, and it was not until Rex rounded the brick wall that he came upon the body. He gave a start, much as Mrs. Willington must have done before him.

The aunt from Wales lay twisted on the ground, her mauve dress hiked above her knees revealing a beige satin slip. A pool of drying blood formed a halo around her dark hair, and out of her pale face stared a pair of lifeless brown eyes.

"She's dead," Mrs. Willington confirmed. "I put the mirror of my compact in front of her mouth to check for a breath, although I don't see how even a cat could have survived a fall from that height."

Rex's gaze skimmed up the fort, which rose sixty feet to the parapet. On this south side the brick had mellowed over the years to a lovely russet and was strung with ivy. No one mounting or descending the steps in the tower would have seen the body unless they were peering out at a downward and sideways angle from one of the arrow slits. Presumably, no one had thought to look through a window in the wing overlooking the patio. Rex's focus returned to the pattern-imprinted concrete where Aunt Gwen must have died upon impact.

"Did you touch anything?" he asked Mrs. Willington, who stood back a short distance, arms crossed and hugging her sides as if she were cold, which she might very well be in her lightweight green suit.

"Of course I didn't touch anything. I watch enough TV to know better than to contaminate a possible crime scene."

"You don't think it was an accident?"

"I shouldn't think so. Have you been up to the battlements?"

Rex shook his head.

"If you had, you'd know it's not that easy to fall off. I wonder what the silly woman was doing up there." Mrs. Willington fumbled with a half-smoked cigarette and lighter, turning aside to shield the flame from the wind. "I snuck out for a ciggie. I was pacing up and down the patio and happened to stroll around the wall of the fort. This was the last thing I expected to find." She inhaled long and hard on the filter and blew out the smoke in an abrupt puff. "Victoria had hoped to hold the reception on the lawn, which would have been lovely. But the weather has been so unpredictable."

That's not the only thing, Rex thought.

"Penny Thompson at the tennis club held her daughter's reception under a marquee in the garden," Mrs. Willington went on, jerking her cigarette about in the air. "I wasn't able to attend, as Tom and I were abroad, but I saw the photos. It was a beautiful May day, unlike today. Only, while the celebrations were going on, someone absconded with Penny's jewels, same as with the snuff boxes. You don't expect people you know to go rummaging around in your bedroom while you're busy hosting a party, do you? Luckily, Penny's jewels were insured, but it's the sentimental value that counts."

Jocelyn Willington did not strike Rex as being the most sentimental of people, but he nodded receptively.

"And now this!" she exclaimed in outrage, turning on the body, then turning away again sharply.

"Did you tell anyone else?" he asked, scanning the scene. "Your husband maybe?"

"No. I came to you first."

"It must have been a tremendous shock to find the body, but you must inform the constable. He'll want to know why you didn't immediately."

"I told you. He's a baby, and somehow you inspire more confidence."

"Thank you, but he might not see things quite that way." Rex guided Mrs. Willington back the route they had come and in through the kitchen.

"I can't believe this has happened, today of all days," she lamented. "Victoria put so much effort into the wedding preparations before she came down with the poisoning. That's what I was mulling over just before I almost tripped over the body."

84

They reached the interior door to the great hall.

"Did you know the aunt at all?" Rex asked, pausing to open it.

"I'd heard about her, but today was the first time I met her. Did you see how she was trying to get her claws into my husband?" Mrs. Willington suddenly remembered her cigarette and found an ashtray in which to stub it out.

"You make her sound like a femme fatale," Rex said with a modicum of amusement, recalling the jolly woman who had put him in mind of a bouncing Indian rubber ball.

"She was swooning all over Tom. It was embarrassing for everybody."

Tom Willington was a handsome man, but Aunt Gwen had flirted with him and Roger Litton as well. "Och, I don't think she meant any harm. She was just having a good time." Until someone decided to end her enjoyment once and for all.

"I take your point. One mustn't speak ill of the dead." Bracing herself, Mrs. Willington went off to seek the constable.

Rex wanted to explore the top of the fort while he still had the chance. The police might arrive in force at any moment and cordon it off. A quick foray could possibly shed some light on the mysterious circumstances of the widow's death.

Mrs. Willington facilitated his plan when she loudly announced to the constable and thereby everyone in the hall that she had witnessed a dead body. While all eyes were riveted on her, Rex ducked into the shadowy mouth of the stairwell and climbed the narrow winding steps. Worn in the center from over a century and a half of use, they were squared off on the outer sides at the fort's west wall.

The stair, Rex saw, was constructed as a left-handed helix. In olden days, this would put an assailant coming up the steps at a disadvantage, by forcing him to fight with his sword hand close to the central pillar, while the defender above him had space by the outer wall in which to maneuver. Rex parried and thrust with his right arm, lumbering about like a dancing bear, and found the design theory to be sound.

Unable to see beyond the next turn, he continued his steep ascent. Dim lamps in wrought iron cages cast eerie shapes upon the stepped ceiling twirling above his head. From the crumbling stone seeped the musty chill odor of an old church. The "Folly" had never been inhabited prior to the wing extensions and had served no useful purpose that Rex could see other than to impress old Cornelius' friends and neighbors and provide a venue for jousting events, and perhaps a good view over the surrounding countryside.

By the time he reached the fourth arrow slit window, he was panting and perspiring. He paused to loosen his tie. As he approached the top, he felt a draught coursing down the stairwell. Daylight illuminated the final sweep of steps, which culminated in an uneven stone landing curving around the central pillar, where he came to a solid oak door standing ajar in the wall.

He pushed the door all the way open and, stooping beneath the low lintel, stepped onto a cobblestone roof. Walled in by a parapet bristling with turrets and abutting the stairwell tower, it offered nowhere to hide. Nor was there much to see: a pair of weathered deck chairs whose striped canvas flapped in the wind, and an abandoned dovecote where a handful of moist crumbs had been scattered within the white wood confines. On the roof's west corner squatted the small stairwell tower he had exited, topped by a flagpole streaming a faded fork-tongue banner. Rex faced the moisture-laden breeze and filled his lungs with fresh air as he took in the panorama, quelling his acrophobia.

Dotted with copses and farms, a patchwork of fields in vibrant yellow and sludgy green melted into misty hills rolling into the distance. Beyond the iron gates of Newcombe Court, the narrow road that had brought the wedding procession to the manor-fort receded into the countryside. The rooftop proved a good look-out post, and Uncle Bobby would have spotted the ambulance while it was still miles away, just as Rex could see, fast approaching from the direction of Derby, the flashing emergency lights of two tiny squad cars.

The scalable stone wall, extending around the property to the gates, hemmed in a perimeter of oak, sycamore and horse chestnut, affording cover for anyone intent on concealing themselves. Walking back to the far corner of the parapet, he peered over a turret. Directly below stretched the back terrace onto which Aunt Gwen had fallen and cracked her skull, and where she sprawled like a dropped rag doll. From this height the scene lacked a sense of reality in spite of the splash of scarlet on concrete. Rex closed his eyes and reopened them to make sure his mind was not playing tricks.

Assailed by sudden vertigo, Rex straightened and pulled back from the wall, resisting the perverse impulse to throw himself into the air. It was a few minutes before he recovered his equilibrium and was able to make some clear-headed observations.

Aunt Gwen, just shy of five foot in heels, would barely have been able to see over the parapet, far less fall off it, unless she had climbed up for some obscure reason and slipped. Furthermore, her portly proportions would not have fit between the closely spaced turrets.

It therefore became apparent to Rex that, unless she had decided to commit suicide at her niece's wedding, Gwendolyn Jones had been forced over the battlements with malice aforethought.

DOUBTS AND SUSPICIONS

POLICE SIRENS BLURTED IN the distance, the two squad cars making slow progress in the mud. Rex, having completed his search of the roof, retreated to the tower steps and began his descent. By the time he returned to the hall, the atmosphere had changed dramatically. A sense of survivors of a shipwreck rallying together and making the best of the situation no longer prevailed. Aunt Gwen's death had changed all that. People now viewed each other with increased suspicion, watchful and tight-lipped, their postures rigid and guarded. Quite possibly, news of the vicar's demise had spread too.

Rex took a seat beside the DJ at his music station. One hand propped under his chin, elbow on the armrest of his chair, he gazed in mute inquiry at Rex, waiting for the latter to speak.

"You've been here pretty much since the end of the banquet, haven't you?" Rex asked.

"Yeah, but I didn't see nothing, if that's what you're asking. I was busy making sure everything was ready for when the dancing began."

"Did you see a short, dark-haired woman go up these steps?"

"Well, yeah. Why'd you want to know?"

"Was she alone?"

"The fat one in the floaty mauve dress?"

"Aye, Gwendolyn Jones."

"She was with that bald bloke with a polka-dot bowtie."

"They went up together?"

"Yeah, but that's all I know. Like I said, I was busy."

"Did you see this man come down?"

The DJ thought for a second. "Can't remember. A few people went up and down, but I couldn't tell you who or when. To be honest, I don't pay much attention. I just do my routine and try to make sure everyone has a blast and remembers DJ Smoothie. Most of my business comes from referrals."

"Is this your main job?"

"Yeah, I get more bookings than I know what to do with in summer and around Christmas time. Any idea when I can split? I'm dead bored waiting around for the fuzz."

"They're on their way."

"Think anyone would mind if I spun some songs?"

"Probably not appropriate under the circumstances."

"I know what you mean, but I still expect to be paid when Mrs. Newcombe gets out of hospital."

Rex left the DJ lolling morosely in his armchair. Jocelyn Willington's husband accosted him as he made his way to the center of the great hall.

"Mr. Graves, did you find anything up top?"

"If you mean clues, nothing much," Rex fudged. "Perhaps a forensics team will have better luck."

"Fancy my wife stumbling on the body." Mr. Willington's light gray eyes scanned the people sitting around the fireplaces. "The murderer must be in the room, unless someone snuck in when no one was looking and pushed that poor woman off the tower."

"Chances are that someone enticed her up there. Somehow, I can't imagine her choosing to go up there alone."

"She might have gone up for some fresh air and exercise."

"She would have got that, all right. I was almost out of breath when I reached the top. Those steps are steep."

"Gwen drank a fair amount of champagne," Diana Litton, the history teacher, interjected, detaching herself from her husband at the refreshment table. "She could have got it into her head to go up and admire the view."

"Can either of you remember when you last saw her?" Rex asked.

Willington shook his head. "I spoke to her before the buffet. After that, I wasn't paying much attention."

"I saw her during the cutting of the cake," Diana replied. "There was quite a bit of activity then, so I'm not sure who was there, but I do remember her refusing any and me wishing I had her self-control."

"Right," Rex concurred. "Mrs. Newcombe was serving the cake. I remember the bride and groom sharing some. Mabel was there, so too was the vicar, and your wife," he told Willington. "There were a lot of people standing around."

"Gwen wasn't around when Polly collapsed," Diana Litton supplied. "Nor was Timmy. That was about half an hour after the cake was cut."

"The ambulance came at two forty-five," Mr. Willington contributed to the timeline. "I kept looking at my watch because I was getting anxious about Polly and her mother's condition."

"Mr. Carter went up to the tower roof to look out for the ambulance," Diana recalled. "Aunt Gwen may have met her death by then. Or shortly afterwards," she added meaningfully.

Rex wondered if she knew her husband had been seen going up the tower steps with Aunt Gwen. He would confront Roger Litton about it at the first available opportunity. "Carter wouldn't have seen her body if he was facing the road. He would have had to be looking directly over the turrets onto the patio on the south side."

"If we could find out who pushed the Welsh woman, we might have a good idea who poisoned the Newcombes and the vicar with arsenic. Mr. Carter admitted it was arsenic," Willington added, intercepting Rex's narrowed gaze. "And not the naturally occurring kind."

Not exactly discreet of Carter, Rex thought, but he saw no point in denying it. "I agree the two might be related. The poisoning would have been a bit hit-and-miss, but the assault on Mrs. Jones was direct and deliberate. Always assuming she was pushed and it wasn't an accident or suicide. How long has Timmy been in your employ, Mr. Willington?"

"Less than a year. He works as a junior accountant. Timmy is hardworking and has a head for figures. He does seem to have a morbid interest in his health, though. Last week he took off early to get a flu shot, and he keeps hand sanitizer on his desk, which is something the female staff do. I don't mean to sound sexist..."

"That's his mother's influence," Diana put in.

"Timmy's ambitious," Willington added. "He's talking about becoming an actuary."

"Isn't that where they calculate risk and probability and all that gubbins?" Diana asked.

"So that life insurance firms can more safely gamble on their clients' longevity, among other things." Willington turned to Rex. "Might be interesting to know who benefits in this case, don't you think?"

"Certainly. I'll ask the family solicitor."

Bobby Carter would be the very person to ask. He appeared informed on every aspect of the Newcombes' business; in fact, intimately so.

AT THAT POINT, PC DIMLEY and Jocelyn Willington reappeared, and Mr. Willington excused himself to join his wife.

"Talk of beneficiaries and arsenic has made me think of something," Diana told Rex. "Did you know that in the fifteenth and sixteenth centuries, members of the European nobility—most notoriously, the Borgias—resorted to arsenic to kill off their rivals? It was so widely used for getting rid of family members it came to be known as 'inheritance powder.' Same symptoms as cholera, which was prevalent at the time, so it was very convenient. And, as there was no way to test for arsenic poisoning back then, malfeasance couldn't be proved."

"Your historical take is most interesting," Rex said. "The Romans used it too. So you think this is a family-related murder?"

"It's a wedding. How much *more* family can you get? Maybe someone didn't want to wait for Aunt Gwen to pop off in her natural time and, when the arsenic failed, resorted to another method. How did you pick up on the arsenic in the first place?"

"A pharmacologist once described the symptoms in graphic detail in court. The shocked reactions of the jury were such that the judge called for an adjournment to give them time to recover. Hard to believe anyone here would purposefully inflict that kind of suffering. And at a wedding, of all things."

Elaine sidled up to them. "Mr. Graves, um, Jeremy wanted me to ask if there was any news..." The girl bit into her lip, flushing all over her face. Her lashes, pale almost to the point of invisibility, gave her bulging eyes the impression of a permanent stare.

"Why didn't your boyfriend come over himself? Better still, he could ask the constable."

Elaine's white fingers pressed into her bottled water, causing the plastic to crackle. "Jeremy and I drew straws."

She gazed abashedly at her shoes, and Rex relented. "Well, lass, as you surely know by now, the vicar succumbed to poisoning. We're waiting on news of the Newcombes. As far as Polly's aunt is concerned, it looks like she, ehm, fell or was pushed off the tower. Did you know her?"

Elaine gulped, though she had not taken as much as a sip from her bottle of water. "I'd never met her before. This is my first visit to Newcombe Court. I only know Polly through Jeremy, because he's friends with Timmy. We went out to the pub as a foursome a couple of times. Timmy and Polly are going to live here, in the spare wing," the girl babbled on nervously. "Polly told me all about the nursery. Do you know how long we're all going to have to stay here? It's been ages."

"That depends on the police."

As if on cue, two detectives in creased suits and a second mud-spattered constable pushed their way through the great hall. Rex deduced they'd had to make an emergency stop, to change a tire or dislodge one of the vehicles from the mire. PC Dimley went to consult with them as Elaine scurried back to Jeremy.

The next moments saw a flurry of activity. The freckle-faced detective, with ginger hair like Rex's own, before his had begun to fade to the shade of sandstone, disappeared into the caterers' wing of the house with Dimley, after thanking everybody not to broadcast news of the events on their phones until the police had finished conducting their business. A bit late for that, Rex thought.

The second detective, a heavyset man with buckled teeth, as though a heavy fist or crowbar had caved them in, gave instructions to the new constable, who proceeded to circulate the room requesting the guests' car keys and explaining that all vehicles had to be searched for the missing antiques.

"Oh, dear," Helen said, rooting in her bag. "They'll have to sift through the junk in my boot. I was going to clear it out last weekend."

"I'm sure they won't issue a ticket for a messy boot," Rex assured her.

She relinquished the keys to the constable, who made a note by her name. "Helen d'Arcy, 19 Barley Close, Derby. Blue Renault," he stated.

"That's correct."

"And your passengers?"

"Mr. Rex Graves here. And a young couple, Meredith Matthews and Reggie Cox."

"I've got those names on the list. Two Reginalds."

Rex only used his christened name on forms, having gone by Rex since age eleven when he discovered that "Reginald" was derived from the Latin *rex*, meaning "king." Unburdened of his fusty old name, he had felt freer to become his own person, and even now cringed at being referred to as Reginald.

The constable addressed him. "I see from PC Dimley's notes that you live in Edinburgh and are visiting Ms. d'Arcy for the weekend. No personal connection to the family that lives here."

"None whatsoever."

"Lucky you're here, isn't it, sir? You being in the business of murder, as it were."

"My profession isn't usually described that way, but I suppose you're right up to a point. I prosecute criminals who commit the most heinous of crimes, including murder."

"I was referring to your sleuthing activities, Mr. Graves. I read about your case down in Sussex with great interest. The article was in *Private Detective*."

"I'm not familiar with the article," Rex said, making a mental note to seek out a back issue of the publication forthwith. "But I'd be happy to help out here."

Helen shot him a raised eyebrow, as if to say, *I just bet you would.*

"I'll let Detectives Lucas and Dartford know. We're a bit short-handed as you can see."

"I was wondering aboot that."

"We've been investigating the latest in a string of burglaries north of here. We responded to this emergency as quickly as we could once arsenic trioxide poisoning was confirmed by the hospital, following your tip. DI Lucas has gone to inform Robert Carter of the death of Victoria Newcombe."

Helen gasped in shock. "She's dead?"

"I'm afraid so, ma'am. Did you know her well?"

"Her daughter attended the school where I work. This was the first time I ever saw Victoria in a social capacity. How is Polly?"

"I can only assume that she has survived the ordeal so far or else we would have been notified."

"She's expecting, you know. You must catch the monster that did this."

"I assure you we'll do everything within our power, ma'am."

"Can I see your list of guests, PC ...?" Rex asked.

"Perrin, sir," the constable replied, obliging him.

"Thanks. I only know some of these people by their first name." Rex scanned the notes, filling in some of the blanks on the spiral pad he carried on him. Helen had bought him a voice recorder for Christmas but he didn't trust it not to break down and omit to register his verbal notes. He returned the list, and the constable moved away and asked Dudley Thorpe for his car keys.

"I didn't nick anything," Timmy's twin objected. "And I don't want anyone touching my Miata. I just waxed it."

"You can accompany PC Dimley and myself, and watch while we perform the search," the constable said amiably yet firmly, giving Dudley little option but to comply.

"Polite young man, that constable," Helen said as the trio moved toward the front door. "And pretty sharp. I don't know why people have to react so abusively when the police are just trying to do their job. Oh, my God, that's three deaths with Victoria. First the vicar, then Aunt Gwen. Now this. I wonder who will break the news to Polly."

"Carter doesn't look like he's up to it at present," Rex remarked when he saw Carter emerge from the manor wing in the company of the freckly detective. Crumpled in upon himself, Polly's uncle seemed to have aged ten years.

"Hopefully, the police will find those snuff boxes and we'll learn who's responsible for the murders," Helen said with indignation. "They must be related."

"If only it might be that simple." Rex knew from experience that premeditated crimes rarely were.

At that juncture he heard vehicles on the gravel outside, followed by a series of car doors slamming. A forensics team in white overalls trooped through the front entrance. They certainly had their work cut out for them, Rex reflected wryly.

Arsenic, blood, skull fragments. A positive field day. And, despite a niggling premonition that morning, the worst he had dreaded was disco-dancing and boredom.

Nothing could have been further from the truth.

AFTER CONFERRING WITH THE head of the crime scene detail, Detective Inspector Lucas wandered over to Rex and stuck out a speckled hand. "Your reputation precedes you," he said. Up close, the freckles on his clean-shaven face merged in places to form patches of orange, matching his hair.

"Thank you," Rex said, pleased that the inspector had sought him out of his own volition. "How are you getting on with the burglaries young Perrin said you were pursuing?"

"There are, admittedly, peculiar difficulties with regard to the crimes."

"Such as?" Rex inquired politely.

"No ruddy evidence. These burglars are pros. No one sees 'em coming or going. There's never any evidence of a break-in, never any mess. We thought the state of the economy was driving some of these wealthy people to commit insurance fraud and claim on items that had never been stolen in the first place, but that doesn't appear to be the case. A flat screen TV fitting the owner's description, down to a tiny scratch in the plasma, turned up at a pawn shop in Nottingham. But so far we've been unable to get a lead on the individual who received cash for the item."

"You think the theft at Newcombe Court may be related?"

"Not sure. Two burglaries in two days hasn't happened before." The inspector rattled something in his pocket; a tube of Smarties or Tic Tacs? "And only the antique snuff box collection seems to have been taken here. Why not the TVs and paintings? Some of them are worth a bob or two. Course, moving the big stuff unobserved at a wedding reception would be well-nigh impossible. Perhaps they were waiting until later to finish the job. We're searching the residence and vehicles right now. You arrived when today?"

"In time for the church service in Aston. My fiancée and I, and two of the guests, came straight here afterwards with everyone else."

"Did you notice anything unusual at the reception?"

"Nothing, until Polly collapsed."

"I take it you were the first person Jocelyn Willington notified about Mrs. Jones' death?" The inspector leveled shrewd blue eyes at Rex, taking his measure.

"The constable was busy with the poisoning and theft. I did suggest she speak to him." Wanting to keep a few cards up his sleeve, Rex decided not to mention yet to the inspector that the DJ had seen Roger Litton go up the tower steps with Gwendolyn Jones. And he doubted DJ Smoothie would volunteer the information himself and risk being detained any longer than necessary. He made a mental note to talk to the teacher next, to see if there was any truth in what the DJ had said.

"Well, first things first," the inspector said. "When Polly Newcombe collapsed, what was your first reaction?"

"I thought her contractions had begun. Then, when her mother and the vicar succumbed to similar symptoms, I knew it had to be poisoning of some kind."

"Were you able to pinpoint the source of the poisoning?"

"I suspect it was the wedding cake."

"Based on?"

"For one thing, after the ambulance took the three victims away, I returned to the reception room, and the miniature figures of the bride and groom had been removed from the top tier, which makes me think someone might have tampered with the evidence during my absence."

"SOCO will bag up samples."

"I doubt that will reveal much. The crumbs are gone from the top tier and the foil base was probably replaced."

"You believe the arsenic was confined to the top tier?" That unnerving dry rattle again in the inspector's pocket, which Rex found peculiarly distracting.

"The bride, mother, and vicar were served first, from the top tier."

"What about Robert Carter, the solicitor?" Lucas asked.

"He didn't eat any cake."

Lucas made a note in his pad. "Would he have been considered family, do you think?"

"He gave Polly away and she calls him 'Uncle Bobby.' He would have been among the first to be served, along with the vicar."

"Your theory fits in with the witness statements so far, and the time sequence. Arsenic trioxide is a fast-acting compound. It's also tasteless, odorless, and white, and could easily be mixed in with the icing. But who did the mixing, eh?" The inspector manically shook whatever it was he had stashed in his pocket. "Robert Carter's grief seemed genuine enough when I informed him of Victoria Newcombe's death. Appears they were quite close."

Appearances can be deceiving, Rex thought, glancing about the room where the guests sat about tensely. He gave a reassuring wave to Helen, who sat with Diane, the history teacher.

Inspector Lucas turned to address them. "Did anyone take the bride and groom figures from the cake? There may be a sentimental reason for doing so. No guilt will be inferred."

When no one spoke, he told Rex in a low voice, "That seems to indicate someone has something to hide. Who else was in the reception room apart from the victims when the miniatures were still there?"

"Diana Litton and Meredith Matthews. Mrs. Litton was a caregiver to her ailing mother. Meredith is a nurse's aide."

Detective Lucas barked out their names. All eyes turned to the startled women as he asked them to turn out their pockets and the contents of their handbags. Rex would have liked to see what it was the inspector kept in his pocket.

He rejoined Helen. Slumped in the armchair in her cornflower-blue suit, she had lost her dewy freshness of the morning, and looked in dire need of reviving.

"I wish we could go home," she said. "I never expected to be here so long. And looking through Diane's handbag is a waste of time. She's the last person who would steal anything."

"She and Meredith were in the room around the time the miniatures went missing, and the police have to start somewhere."

Rex thought Clive more suspect, however. He clung to Jasmina, who seemed anxious now to get away from his clutches. This made him blink all the more. Most of the guests appeared fidgety as tension built in the hall.

DIANA LITTON PRODUCED A bunch of keys, a compartmentalized wallet stacked with bank and library cards, a transparent topped fuchsia lipstick, and a wad of clean tissues. Meredith came up with a comb, a retro clip-purse, lip balm, and breath mints.

Most of the spectators looked disappointed that nothing incriminating had been found. Others were affronted when asked to empty their own pockets and purses. Jasmina in her clinging sequined number patently had nowhere in her clothes to hide anything. PC Dimley, recalled from searching the vehicles, made a clumsy attempt to pat her down all the same, eliciting shocked giggles from the thusly assaulted girl, who stared in wide-eyed entreaty at Clive.

"Watch where you put your hands, you inept clodhopper," he snapped, one movement away from completing a punch in the constable's reddening face.

While the detectives questioned Diana and the young nurse's aide, Rex caught up with Roger Litton at the refreshment table as he was helping himself to coffee.

The Home Ec teacher took a tentative sip from his cup. "Tastes all right. Need something to keep me awake."

"Roger, I hope you don't think me a busybody, but someone mentioned seeing you go up the tower steps with the Welsh lady. Did you mention that fact to either of the detectives?"

Litton flushed to the top of his bald spot. "Well, no, I didn't, actually. I only went part of the way. Up the steps, I mean." He blushed a deeper shade of pink. "It's quite a climb up those winding stairs and she was dragging on my arm. I made my excuses and let her continue without me. Chivalry only extends so far, you know."

"Did she mention why she wanted to go to the roof?"

"She said the view was breathtaking. The climb alone took my breath away. No view is worth a stroke."

"Or a broken neck."

"Quite so. Sorry I can't help you there."

"Any indication she was going to meet someone?" Rex asked in a final attempt to discover why the aunt had gone up the tower stairs. Could it really have been for the view on such a dismal day?

Roger Litton shook his head thoughtfully. "She was babbling away about this and that, and I ceased paying much attention. I say, what's going on over there?"

Rex turned. The older crowd was grouped on one side of the fireplace, giving a wide berth to Detective Dartford's prodigious posterior as he bent over the hearth. Surgical gloves molded to his hands, he held his tie to his chest to prevent it from catching alight while he prodded in a far corner of the fireplace with an iron poker.

"Ey-up," he announced to himself.

Among the pile of ashes, Rex spotted two blackened figures, melted and misshapen, but still recognizable as the missing plastic bride and groom. Detective Lucas, who had finished interviewing Diana Litton, watched as Dartford fished them out of the fireplace.

"You were right," he said, approaching Rex. "Someone got rid of them. Our suspect, more likely than not."

"Was Mrs. Litton able to shed any light on the miniatures?"

"She left the room once Victoria Newcombe had been taken out on a stretcher. Said she wanted to go and wash her hands. Meredith Matthews escorted the vicar to the ambulance. Someone could have gone in then to get rid of any traces of arsenic. With so many people in the house and all the commotion, it's hard to know who was where. Seems most of the guests crowded around the main entrance when the ambulance arrived."

"The poisoner would have realized that once the police got here, there would be no chance of going back into the banquet room."

"Precisely. Forensics won't be able to confirm the existence of arsenic in the wedding cake if the evidence was removed, so we only have your hypothesis that it was in the cake in the first place. Here are the facts: The cake was in the kitchen this morning waiting to be iced. Stella Pembleton worked as a pastry chef at Price's Bakery in Derby before starting her own business. But she's not the only person who could have mixed in the poison. Her sister and niece were also here this morning, as were the two servers hired for the day. No priors on any of them. We called the station and ran a check."

The inspector proceeded to consult his notes. "Pollard, the bartender, twenty-six years of age, lives alone in Derby. Drake, forty-two, serves at the buffet table, a family man from Aston. Rachel, Lydia Pembleton's daughter, is a student at the University of Derby and works for the catering business part-time. Don't see any of them risking their jobs to jolly up a party with a lethal dose of arsenic. The DJ came too late to have tampered with the cake, which was already iced by then. Always assuming it was the cake that had the arsenic in it, but I'm holding to that opinion since it was the surest thing that everyone would eat. Some people are vegetarians, others are allergic to shellfish, others don't like avocados. You get my drift."

"Aye, it's tradition to eat cake at a wedding," Rex added, supporting his argument that the inspector now seemed to have adopted as his own.

"So, if it was the cake, the catering staff had opportunity, as did the people at the house this morning. Polly, Mrs. Newcombe, Mabel Thorpe, Robert Carter," the inspector listed from his notes.

"And Amber, the maid of honour. She spent the night here."

"Must have missed that," Lucas said, flipping back through his pages, clearly miffed. "Odd sort of girl. Got the impression she has some sort of chip on her shoulder. Still, can't be easy being a young single mum. As for the other family members, Timothy and Dudley Thorpe were in Aston this morning, Timothy at his mother's house where he still lives, and Dudley Thorpe with his wife. I never met such an arrogant ponce." The inspector, evidently remembering his position, quickly forged on with his review. "It's unlikely

Polly or Victoria Newcombe accidentally poisoned themselves. That would seem to limit possible suspects to eight, unless someone snuck in."

"Agreed," Rex said. "The two caterers and the three staff, Amber, Bobby Carter, and Mabel Thorpe all had access to the cake. Sticking by our theory, that takes care of opportunity. But what about motive?"

"I think we can assume the vicar's death was unintentional, unless someone had a specific grievance against him and was prepared to kill a pregnant girl and a middle-aged woman as collateral damage. But then there's the aunt as well, killed by other means."

"I don't think Victoria Newcombe would have liked to be referred to as middle-aged," Rex remarked. "She certainly didn't look it."

"I only saw her in an unflattering hospital gown with tubes snaking out of her." Lucas passed a hand wearily across his freckled face. "Hope the daughter makes it. She was being prepped for the operating room when we got there."

A polite cough from PC Perrin interrupted them. "Inspector, the coroner is here."

"About time," Lucas grumbled. "Just as well he only attends to patients who are already dead. What's going on round back?"

"The patio's been cordoned off and a tent placed over the body," the constable reported. "Looks like rain, but SOCO* has finished processing the area."

"Right, I'll be out directly. Any luck with the snuff boxes?"

"No, sir."

---

* Scene of crime officer.

Rex had his own ideas in that regard, having had time to mull over the day's events, but decided to keep those ideas to himself for the time being on the off chance he was wrong.

REX LOOKED ACROSS THE hall to where the young guests either sat around aimlessly or else frenetically texted on their phones. He considered each in turn as potential suspects. Jeremy and his girl-friend, Elaine, had driven straight from Derby to the church service in Aston-on-Trent. Ditto Reggie and Meredith, who had come up from London by train. Little chance those four had tampered with the cake.

Taking advantage of Mabel's temporary absence, Rex approached Timmy Thorpe once more. "Do you mind?" he asked, indicating the chair vacated by the groom's mother.

"Go ahead," Timmy replied, somewhat revived since Rex had last spoken to him. "I just heard that I have a son, safely delivered as of fifteen minutes ago."

"Congratulations!"

"Son and heir to Newcombe Court," Dudley jeered.

"He's in an incubator, but doing well," Timmy explained, ignoring his brother.

"And your wife?" Rex inquired.

"Not out of the woods yet. The doctor performed a caesarean earlier than scheduled because the baby was showing signs of fetal distress. I'm going to the hospital now. My mother is getting her hat. A dad. I can hardly believe it."

"How are you feeling?"

"Drained."

Timmy looked it. Dark rings, accentuated by an unhealthy pallor, circled his washed-out blue eyes.

"Timmy, I wanted to ask how much cake you ate."

"Just a forkful. I was feeling a bit queasy."

"What about you, Dudley?"

"What sort of daft question is that?"

"If you could just answer the question?" Rex said curtly, out-staring him.

"I didn't have any, did I? I already told you that. I don't have a sweet tooth. My body is my temple and all that. I don't fill it with junk." He gave Rex a look implying that perhaps the large Scotsman should reassess what he put into his own temple.

"Are you saying the arsenic was in the wedding cake?" Timmy asked.

Dudley rolled incredulous eyes. "That's exactly what he's saying, you daft pillock. Haven't you been listening?" Dudley turned to Rex. "He has a head for figures but not much else."

"Who would do that?" Tears welled in Timmy's eyes.

"That's what we're trying to ascertain. Any ideas?"

"It had to have been an accident."

"I'd ask those Pembleton sisters," Dudley suggested.

"I have."

112

"Course, if it was them, they did Timmy here a whopping great favour getting rid of his mum-in-law. Wish I could be so lucky."

"Shut up, Dud."

"Don't pretend you're not pleased about it," Dudley said, apparently not caring who heard. "Now you have this whole place to yourself."

"Just piss off." Timmy's face had turned an unhealthy red and his eyes bulged with fury.

"Shame about the vicar, though," his brother went on. "Still, he was getting on."

"Have you no feelings?" Timmy asked querulously.

"Don't be so soft." Dudley jumped out of his armchair and stalked off in the direction of the refreshment table.

"No love lost between you two, I see," Rex commiserated.

"Do you have brothers?" Timmy asked.

"I'm an only child."

"Lucky you."

"Didna feel that way growing up. My mother had me late in life and it was like being brought up by a grandmother."

Timmy nodded in comprehension. Mabel Thorpe stood before a heavily framed mirror fastening on her cloche hat with a large metal pin. She cut a rather prim and timid figure. Ignoring Rex, she joined her son, and together they made for the entrance, Timmy walking with his hands cupped in loose fists at chest level, as though anticipating a blow or else reluctant to take up another person's space. The young man clearly lacked confidence. He was at the mercy of the world—and, evidently, a person or persons in it.

As mother and son left by the front entrance, Rex glimpsed two figures in white lift a black body bag into the back of a white panel van. Poor Aunt Gwen. She had arrived in a party dress for her niece's wedding, little suspecting the gruesome fate awaiting her at Newcombe Court.

Lucas stepped into the great hall. "Broken neck, the coroner confirmed. The autopsy might tell us more. A note was found on the body." The excitement in the inspector's voice contradicted his impassive expression.

"A suicide note?" Rex asked in surprise.

Lucas showed Rex a slip of white paper protected within a transparent bag. "*Meet me at the top of the tower. An admirer,*" it read in a scrawled hand.

"An assignation," Rex corrected himself. "That explains why she went up to the rooftop."

"It was stuffed down her brassiere. If only we knew who wrote it. We could get handwriting samples, but if the intention was to bump off Gwendolyn Jones, the perp would likely have disguised his writing."

"I wonder if she knew her admirer."

"If only the dead could speak! The bartender claims the note was left on his tray when his back was turned. The name 'Gwen' is jotted on the other side." Lucas flipped the plastic bag so Rex could see. "After inquiring who Gwen was, the bartender delivered it to her."

"Is there any record of anyone being seen descending the tower after the cake-cutting?"

"That's when people started dropping like flies. The guests' memories are a blur."

114

"The DJ saw Roger Litton escort the Welsh woman up the stairs," Rex imparted. "But Litton told me he didn't go to the top and he can't remember if she mentioned meeting someone."

"We'll have to dig into all these people's backgrounds." The inspector looked decidedly frazzled, his freckles about ready to pop off his face. He extracted a plastic container of aspirin from his coat pocket and proceeded to munch on a handful of pills. One mystery solved, Rex thought with wry amusement. But what of the murders and missing snuff boxes?

He decided to help out in one matter, whether his assistance had been requested or not.

BOXED IN

REX FOUND HELEN STANDING among the cluster of teachers from her school and told her to keep her fingers crossed that his hunch, which he was about to act upon, did not blow up in his face.

"What hunch?" she asked.

"It has to do with those two love birds, Clive and Jasmina."

In point of fact, the pair seemed far less lovey-dovey now, but then everyone appeared more jaded. He drew the svelte beauty aside, while Helen looked on in curiosity.

"I wonder if you would permit me to look inside your gift box."

Jasmina's eyes widened. "Excuse me?"

"Your wedding gift."

Asking Helen and Clive to accompany them, he led the three guests into the reception room, where he bade them stand inside the door, out of the way of the forensics team who were packing up their equipment, while he made for the table of unopened wedding presents.

"Whatever it is you're up to, you'd better be right," Helen warned after him in a low voice. "I have to work with Clive, remember."

"This is yours, is it not?" Rex asked Jasmina, returning from the table and handing her a large box.

Hesitantly she untied the ribbon and lifted the lid. Rex looked inside. The box was empty, save for a few remnants of scrunched tissue paper.

"What was in here?"

"A fruit bowl."

"Where is it now?"

"I have no idea."

"I have an idea." Rex took the trio into the caterers' temporary kitchen and picked up off the pine table a bowl decorated with a row of pears and cherries. "This looks the right size for the box. Is this the fruit bowl you brought to the wedding?"

"Why—yes," Jasmina replied. "What is it doing here?"

"You tell me." He handed her the bowl. "We got Polly and Timmy a fruit bowl too. Luckily, not the same one."

Jasmina giggled. Rex began to wonder if the high-pitched laughter might be a nervous tic. Even Clive looked disconcerted.

"Why did you need Clive and me there?" Helen asked as they exited the manor wing.

"As witnesses. I suppose I should have cleared it with Inspector Lucas first. The police, sensitive to the occasion, must have been leaving the wedding gifts until last, hoping to find the missing antique collection elsewhere."

"But Jasmina's box was empty. The poor girl is terribly embarrassed. Why pick on her box?"

"It was a long shot, but I saw her stealing down the stairs with it and she was reluctant to accept my offer of assistance."

"I wonder where the snuff boxes are now. And what was Jasmina's bowl doing on the kitchen table?"

"Sometimes it's hard to see the wood for the trees."

"What do you mean?"

Smiling at Helen's confusion, Rex went to find PC Perrin. "Any luck with the snuff boxes?"

"They seem to have walked."

"Nonsense. Snuff boxes don't walk."

"That's not what I meant, sir."

"Where haven't you looked?"

"We've searched everywhere. The cellar, the attic, every knook and cranny."

"Use your brain, lad," Rex said in paternal fashion. "If this was an outside job, the hiding place has to be somewhere familiar. Our criminal wouldn't have had time to go rummaging around looking for a good hiding place."

"But we searched the vehicles thoroughly," the young constable insisted. "The wheel wells, under the seats, you name it. That Dudley Thorpe was right incensed when we poked around the bonnet of his new Miata. He called us PC Plod and PC Dimwit. Dimley gets called that a lot."

"He's a good lad but he'll probably never get off the beat. A smart lad like you, however, could go places."

"I'd love to make detective one day, sir."

"Then dig deeper. What is in the house that wasn't here before?"

"Oh, you mean the mobile ovens and catering boxes with the crockery and glasses? Those are the first places we looked."

"What else was brought into the house?" Rex prompted.

"Well, the DJ's gear, the catering staff's bags, you know, with a change of shirt in case something got spilt."

Rex all but burst at the seams now. "The DJ has quite a sophisticated setup," he reflected aloud. "Mikes, lighting, amps, speakers. Shame he never got to demonstrate their full potential."

Perrin tore off toward the back of the great hall. Within minutes, a cry of triumph resounded. The two detectives dashed over to where the constable kneeled behind a speaker. "Hidden in here, sirs," he told them, holding open a canvas sack. "Dozens of snuff boxes wrapped in paper."

"Good work, Constable," Lucas declared. "Let's see what DJ Smoothie has to say for himself."

"I can't take all the credit, sir," PC Perrin told the retreating inspector. "Mr. Graves gave me a pointer."

"Mr. Graves, you are welcome to sit in, if you like."

"Technically, you found them," Rex told the young constable. "And you need the brownie points more than I do."

"I do appreciate it, sir," Perrin said with a broad grin, turning to follow in the inspector's footsteps.

"I would never have thought to look in the speakers," Helen said, joining Rex.

"More wood, more trees," he said enigmatically.

"Well, good for PC Perrin, I say. He's a lot more switched on than PC Dimbulb."

"Dimley."

"Freudian slip, I assure you," she apologized as Rex strode off after the inspector, eager to see what DJ Smoothie had to say for himself, and about anyone else, for that matter.

INSPECTOR LUCAS TOOK THE suspect into the caterers' kitchen for interviewing. DJ Smoothie looked significantly less smooth than ruffled, his flagging Elvis looks pale and puffy beneath the fluorescent strip lighting. "Now, Harry, how do you explain the snuff boxes turning up in one of your speakers?" the detective asked, seated across the pine table where Rex joined them.

"I want a lawyer."

"Mr. Rex Graves here is a lawyer," the inspector informed him.

"I want my own lawyer," the DJ scoffed, folding his muscular arms. "I know my rights."

"Been down this road before, have you?" Lucas asked. "Then you know it would be in your best interests to cooperate. Murder and robbery are serious crimes."

"I didn't murder nobody."

"I'm inclined to believe you, given that you arrived shortly before the guests."

"So?"

"We think the arsenic was blended with the icing on the wedding cake."

"I had nothing to do with that. I can't bake to save my life."

"Did you see or hear anything that made you suspicious?"

"I just do my job and let others take care of theirs. Smoothie's my name, music's my game."

"Well, now your job is to assist the police with their enquiries."

"I've got nothing to say to you lot."

"You do not have to say anything." Lucas garbled, wearily parroting the rest of the caution without pause or punctuation. "There may be a perfectly rational reason why the snuff boxes were found in your speaker," he added, resuming his caustic tone. "We just haven't sussed out what it is yet."

Harry's mouth remained firmly shut. Inspector Lucas planted his freckled hands on the knotted pine tabletop. "If you copped to the theft and gave us what you know about the arsenic, it could cut your prison time down considerably."

"I told you, I don't know nothing. And I'd never get prison time for a first offense without proof."

"Where did you get that idea? We're not talking about stealing an ice cream cone from off the pier one Sunday afternoon. Those are highly valuable antiques you stashed in your speaker."

DJ Smoothie, who had recovered some of his composure, leaned back in his chair. "I never did. Someone must've put them there. The prisons are overflowing with pedos, druggies, and terrorists. I'd never be sent down on suspicion of nicking some poxy little snuff boxes."

Rex and the inspector exchanged glances. The interview was patently going nowhere. Lucas nodded almost imperceptibly, giving Rex the go-ahead to question Harry.

A prosecutor at the supreme criminal court of Scotland, Rex was a dab hand at questioning suspects and witnesses. "You said something about this being a first offense," he addressed the DJ. "There have been other burglaries in Derbyshire."

"I suppose you're going to try to pin those on me too."

"I'll bet if we had a list of your gigs, we'd find the burglaries took place at or near your venues." Rex turned to Inspector Lucas. "Jocelyn Willington has a tennis friend who was burgled this month during a wedding reception held at her house. Might be worth inquiring if Harry was the DJ on that occasion." He redirected his attention to the suspect whose tensed features betrayed his unease. "I imagine not all the thefts coincide with your gigs. But once you've had a chance to case the homes, you plan an encore—solo this time. Or maybe you prefer duets?"

"What's he on about?" the DJ asked Inspector Lucas.

"TVs, antiques, it's all the same to you, as long as you can find a buyer," Rex went on. "That van of yours is ideal for transporting stolen items. It's a plain white one, right?" Parked in front of Helen's Renault. "Why not advertise your business on it? Too revealing?"

"You have a very creative mind," Harry told him. "Almost as imaginative as Detective Lucas with his ice cream cones. I just haven't got around to putting logos on yet. What do you actually have on me?"

"An accomplice."

123

"Oh, really? Go on, then. This I can't wait to hear." Smirking, the DJ tipped back in his chair, arms crossed and bulging.

"A girl who infiltrates the parties."

"Yeah?"

"The lovely Jasmina. How else do you think we knew where to find the snuff boxes?"

"She never. I mean—" The DJ stopped, too late realizing his mistake.

"She did, Harry. Gave you up to save her own skin."

"You're fibbing! I don't even know her!"

Rex turned to the inspector, who had been following the line of questioning, the tic of an incipient smirk at the corner of his lips. "Should we bring the lady in?"

"By all means." Lucas called to the constable standing guard at the kitchen door. "Perrin! Get Jasmina Patel in here."

The inspector pulled out his container of pills and, cupping a few into his mouth, crunched them as though they were candy, breaking the silence as the three of them waited for the young woman, Harry rubbing bleary eyes in a gesture of defeat.

DJ SMOOTHIE SHOT AN accusatory glance at the young woman as she entered the room.

"Mr. Graves is assisting us in an unofficial capacity," Inspector Lucas informed her. "You may choose not to answer his questions. Or mine for that matter."

"Am I under arrest?"

"Not at this point."

"I think you know what this is all about," Rex addressed Jasmina. "Please take a seat." She did so carefully, as if the chair might disintegrate beneath her negligible weight. "How long have you known Clive Rutherford, the mathematics teacher?"

"A month or so," she said, knitting her smooth brow in puzzlement. Clearly, she had not expected to be questioned about Clive.

"Where did you meet?"

She glanced at the inspector. "Do I have to tell him? This is my private life."

"Just answer the question, please."

"I met him online."

"You have a thing for teachers who enjoy microbrews and long walks in the rain?" Rex inquired.

Jasmina's liquid gaze fixed warily on his face. "It's just that, well, I saw on Facebook that he was single and, you know... He seemed nice," she added lamely.

"And he'd been invited to Mrs. Newcombe's daughter's wedding. You saw the list of invitees at your father's print shop and you singled out the men who didn't have 'and Mrs.' after their name. Then you did a search on the Internet and up popped Clive Rutherford of the lonely hearts club."

Jasmina let slip a glance at Harry. "I don't follow," she murmured.

"It's quite simple," Rex explained. "You and Harry are the real partners. Posing as Clive Rutherford's date, you brought a big box to the wedding, took out the fruit bowl when no one was looking, and left it in the kitchen where it would blend in with the other serving dishes. Then you went upstairs, filled the empty box with the antiques, and brought it back down, which is when I saw you and we had our pleasant little chat." He kept his tone just as benign. Jasmina said nothing, and he continued.

"Since I was following you, you couldn't give Harry the goods just then. So, during the cutting of the cake, when everyone's attention was directed at the bride and groom, you retrieved the box, helped Harry transfer the snuff boxes to the speaker, and then, prevented for some reason from going into the kitchen, put the empty gift box on the reception room table, intending to replace the fruit bowl when the opportunity presented itself. Such an opportunity, however, did not present itself. The bride fell ill and the room was cleared, preventing you from carrying out your plan to its conclusion."

Jasmina remained so silent and still, she could have been carved out of ice.

"Caught red-handed, eh?" the inspector said to the thieves. "It was a daring plan. You couldn't have anticipated a multiple murder taking place on the big day."

"How did you know where to find the snuff boxes?" Rex asked the young woman.

She turned to face him, a lost look on her face. "I don't know what you're talking about."

"Jasmina," the inspector said with a patient sigh. "We're giving you a chance here. I strongly suggest you take it."

The girl flicked frightened eyes at Rex, who nodded in encouragement. "Harry overheard one of the caterers say they were all in the study. He went upstairs and picked the lock." She stole a look at Harry.

"She's lying. She must've put the boxes in the speaker when I wasn't looking."

"That's not true. You picked the lock." Jasmina turned to the inspector. "He was a locksmith before he became a full-time DJ."

Harry groaned and buried his face in his hands.

"Being a mobile disk jockey doesn't pay well?" Rex inquired.

"I had my van to pay off, and I just got some new mixing equipment. Plus Jaz has very expensive tastes. It was her idea to nick stuff. We met at a karaoke I was doing at a bar. There. That's the whole story."

"How did you find out about the snuff box collection?"

"Jaz researched Newcombe Court on the Net to see if it was the sort of place that might contain valuables. She came across an article about the missing owner and a reference to some early nineteenth-century snuff boxes, which we figured must be worth a bob or two."

"My father will be dishonoured," Jasmina broke out. "Is there any way I can fully redeem myself?"

"Your father will be more dishonoured if you go down for murder," the inspector told her.

"Murder?" the young woman wailed. "I had nothing to do with any murder! I would never kill anyone! Never!"

"Greed can make you do things you might never have thought yourself capable of," Lucas said evenly.

"You have no proof I was involved in a murder. Why would I murder any of these people?"

"Have either of you any idea who might have?" Lucas questioned.

"Why should we?" the DJ asked. "If someone hadn't poisoned the food, we'd be home free. Or at least on our way to Europe."

"Except that Robert Carter discovered the items had gone missing," Rex pointed out.

"That was after people started getting sick. What was he doing in the study anyway? It's not his house, far as I know. Freakin' busybody."

"You are going down, Harry," the inspector informed him with a grave shake of his head. "And not just for the snuff boxes. You are looking very good for the string of burglaries in Derbyshire. You being a locksmith by trade explains a lot."

"I haven't confessed to anything. I just meant we were planning a holiday abroad."

128

"If I help, will it get me off the accomplice charge?" Jasmina pleaded, looking at her interrogators in turn.

Rex left it to the inspector to answer.

"If either of you can give us any assistance leading to an arrest in the murders, we'll review each of your cases accordingly. You will also need to give us the name of your fence or fences for the stolen goods."

"Harry took care of that," Jasmina told him. "I just took my cut."

Head bowed between his elbows and rubbing fingers through his slicked-back hair, the DJ swore softly under his breath.

"C'mon, Harry," Lucas said cheerily. "Names, dates, locations. Otherwise, we'll just show your Elvis mug at every pawnshop each side of the River Trent and beyond, if necessary. We'll offer a reward for information and it'll cost us a ton in manpower, so we'll be mightily pissed off by your lack of cooperation when someone recognizes you as being the person who sold them the merchandise off the back of a lorry."

With pained reluctance, Harry supplied the inspector with the relevant information, while Rex asked Jasmina what she had planned to tell Clive after the wedding, when she had no further use for him. "He seems pretty infatuated with you," he remarked.

"Not me with him!" she said pouting. "So boring! After a few weeks, I would have told him it was over or just stopped taking his calls. Helen is much better off with you."

"Thank you."

"Even if you *did* catch me out," she reproached him. She massaged her earlobe, enflamed by the silver hoop. "Cheap fake earrings!" she spat at Harry.

129

Jasmina was so much more alluring when she didn't giggle, Rex thought. Harry raised a fist, before dropping it in a dismissive gesture.

"Now then," the inspector announced when he had finished his note-taking. "Let's see if you can both be as helpful with the murder side of things." He looked first at Jasmina. "Anything you may have noticed out of the ordinary?"

"I really want to help." She wet her lips. "Um, the bride and that pig of a best man, Dudley, had a fight. I heard them when I was upstairs."

"Did you see them?"

"I saw their reflections in a mirror as I crossed the landing to the study. I hid behind the door until they left."

"Did you hear what they were saying?"

"Dudley was talking about someone called Mack and said something about her Uncle Bobby. She said something like, 'It's not true!' She called him a lot of names, and he said, 'I'll murder the bloody lot of you,' and then he stormed out of the room. After I gave Harry the antiques, I couldn't put the bowl back in the gift box because someone was in the kitchen. A man wearing a hooded jacket and gloves. Other than that, I couldn't give a description."

When she finished her recital, the inspector humphed and twiddled his pencil. The reported outburst from Dudley did not surprise Rex, since the young man had a short fuse, judging by his reaction when the police searched his sports car. His threat and the hooded stranger, however, Rex treated with a degree of skepticism. After all, it was in Jasmina's interest to finger someone for the murders at Newcombe Court.

"I remember something else," she added with passion.

130

"Let's be having it," Lucas said, lethargically drumming the eraser end of his pencil on the table.

"Dudley shouted, 'You let your scheming mother and her henchman control your life. My brother is a pawn in their games.'"

"Is that verbatim?" Rex asked.

"Word for word," the inspector told her when she looked nonplussed.

"Oh. Yes, pretty much. I wondered who the henchman was."

Rex turned to the DJ. "You mentioned seeing the Welsh lady go up the tower steps with Roger Litton."

"I don't know their names. He wasn't gone more than five minutes."

"That's not what you told me."

"Now I remember better. They made a comical pair, him with his scrawny neck and bowtie, her short and fat. I was thinking it was just enough time for a quickie. Happens more often than you'd think at weddings, you know."

"Thank you for your observations, Harry," Inspector Lucas said in a deadpan voice. He gazed at the pair of thieves, awaiting further revelations. "If that's all, PCs Dimley and Perrin will take you into custody now."

"Inspector," Jasmina blurted. "Can we go out the back way? I can't face being paraded in handcuffs in front of all those people!"

The inspector acquiesced. As they were led out of the kitchen, he asked Rex how he had come to suspect Jasmina.

"She told me she'd put her gift upstairs for safekeeping. 'Safekeeping' was the word Stella Pembleton used in connection with the snuff boxes, and it just resonated and made me wonder why Jasmina had really gone to the trouble of separating her gift from the rest of the presents. Plus, her relationship with Clive Rutherford seemed staged right from the start. At first I thought he had retained the services of a beautiful escort for the occasion, in order to impress my fiancée. Then when PC Perrin showed me the list with the name Jasmina Patel on it, I remembered Ms. Pembleton mentioning Patel's being the company that had printed up the invitations."

"You canny Scotsman! Well, that's one case closed, thanks in part to you, but we still have the more serious one of the murders to solve."

Rex was glad the inspector had said "we."

"Jasmina may have given us a lead," Lucas went on. "If she's to be believed, Dudley Thorpe had a grouse with the Newcombes. Of course, that stuff about the hooded intruder is probably a load of old cock. Right, well, we'll keep the family here for now. Mrs. Thorpe and her son are returning after their visit to the hospital. It is, after all, Timothy Thorpe's home now."

"Jasmina Patel is not exactly a credible witness," Rex concurred. "But what she said about Bobby Carter rang true."

"At least we found our burglars. That will be a relief to the wealthy folk of Derbyshire."

Rex nodded, pleased for the wealthy folk of Derbyshire. However, he wouldn't be satisfied until he knew the identity of the killer, and he was determined to find out by the end of the day just who that person might be. He could not justifiably stay beyond then, since he was not an official part of the investigation. Not that it was going to stop him.

"YOUR EX-BOYFRIEND WAS HAD," Rex told Helen, who, along with everyone else in the house, had been alerted as to the arrest by some source. She watched from the portcullis window as the two constables escorted Jasmina and DJ Smoothie to the patrol car and installed them in the back seat.

"Imagine falling idiotically in love with a common thief!" Helen remarked. "Perhaps now he'll go back to wearing glasses and stop blinking like a lunatic."

"Don't be too hard on him. We've all made fools of ourselves over a beautiful woman."

"Even you, Rex?"

"I can't rightly recall," he replied evasively.

"Are the police sure she and the DJ had nothing to do with the poisonings?"

"They'll be questioned at the station, but it seems unlikely in view of the circumstances. No obvious motive, for one thing; and little opportunity, for another. Listen, have you seen Bobby Carter anywhere?"

133

"He's outside, pacing the driveway. Before you go, what did you mean earlier about not being able to see the wood for the trees?"

"'There is nothing more deceptive than an obvious fact,' said Sherlock Holmes."

"Rex," Helen warned. "Please stop with all the proverbs and quotes."

"Sorry. But think about it: Jasmina's fruit bowl was lying in full view on the kitchen table. It didn't match the white crockery provided by Pembleton Caterers, but it could have been on loan from Mrs. Newcombe. Later, when I remembered Jasmina carrying a box down the stairs, which I suspected contained the snuff boxes, I wondered where she had hidden the fruit bowl."

"In plain sight."

"Exactly. Same with the snuff boxes. In the middle of the floor in the DJ's speaker."

"How did you guess?"

"I rarely guess, lass. Process of elimination. Everywhere else had been searched. The obvious hiding place was somewhere nobody would notice when it was moved. Mobile DJ—perfect cover."

Leaving Helen to appreciate the logic of Sherlock's observation, Rex stepped out the front door into the bracing fresh air. He reached into his pocket for his pipe, trusting that the peaty vanilla aroma of the Clan tobacco would work its usual charm. Although trying to give up smoking, he kept the pipe handy for an emergency. Even so, he had not anticipated an emergency of such epic proportions.

Quo Vadis—Whither goest thou? the worn-smooth date-stone questioned, compelling him to turn his head mid-stride on the driveway, as though drawn irresistibly by a pair of watching eyes.

I'd certainly like to know where your descendent went, Rex responded in his thoughts. He could not help but feel that Tom Newcombe's disappearance had some bearing on the case.

He found the family solicitor pacing the gravel farther down the driveway, lit cigar in hand, and fell in step beside him. By tacit agreement, they moved away from the vehicles parked outside the manor-fort and made toward the lush purple blooms on the rhododendron hedge by the gate.

"Did you ever try to track down Victoria's husband?" Rex asked after a few moments of silence during which time he resolved not to succumb to his pipe.

"Funny, I was just thinking about him. Yes, we contacted the Salvation Army and other organizations that trace relatives in the UK and overseas. But without a clue as to where he went, it was hard to know where to start. We called everybody he knew, all his acquaintances and his business colleagues in Leicester, where he had his last meeting. Or would have, had he arrived. The police checked hospitals and morgues in the area in case he'd been mugged or run over by a bus."

"Sounds like he didn't want to be found, or else someone didn't want you to find him."

"That's the conclusion we came to and, eventually, Victoria decided to just get on with her life. Except at Christmas and on Polly's birthday, when she'd start wondering all over again. You know how it is. It continues to hang over one."

Like a hangman's noose over the head of a murderer? Rex wondered. "You appear to have been close to Victoria."

"Beyond the scope of my professional involvement with the family, you mean? Yes, we became close when her husband disappeared, but nothing improper, I assure you. And, naturally, I became attached to Polly. She's like a daughter to me."

"She's going to need you all the more now, with her mother gone." Assuming Polly survived her ordeal.

"Victoria gone!" Carter cried hoarsely, slowing to a stop before the perfect purple orbs on the rhododendron hedge. "I can't believe it. I thought maybe in time..." He thumb-flicked the end of his cigar, dislodging the ash. "Well, time ran out for Victoria. Just goes to show..."

He stared back at the fort. "Now that I look at that Latin inscription, which I must have passed under a hundred times without giving it a second thought, it seems to mock my procrastination. One thing's for sure: I'll see that DJ Smoothie rots in prison for the rest of his miserable life. Lucky I checked the study when I went looking for Gwen. I bet he was planning to get away with a much bigger haul. Too much of a coincidence if he didn't poison the cake as well."

"Fact is," Rex said, "no violence was committed during any of the thefts prior to today. Personally, I think we're looking at two unrelated crimes. The theft of the snuff boxes because the DJ had access when the occupants of the house would be busy celebrating the wedding. The murders because the intended victims would be under one roof with enough potential suspects to confuse the police."

"Possibly," Bobby Carter conceded.

"You declined the cake. Why was that?"

"I'm a diabetic, so I avoid sugar. Never thought my condition would actually save my life," the solicitor said in a tone of sobering realization. "But when Gwen failed to fall into the trap of eating the portion of cake reserved for family, another way was found to dispose of her. Pretty diabolical, if you ask me."

"Especially if it was kith or kin who plotted the poisoning," Rex added, pensively tapping the stem of his unlit pipe on his chin, relishing the familiarity of the smooth bowl in his hand.

Carter shuddered as he looked up at the gray battlements delineated against the bleak sky. "Must have required someone of considerable strength to chuck the old girl over the turrets."

"Mr. Carter," Rex inquired, "Who benefits from Gwen's or Victoria's death? Do you know of any life insurance policies in effect?"

"No. Victoria's will leaves everything to Polly and her offspring, assuming Thomas Newcombe stays out of the picture. Should he ever reappear, he is entitled to the estate, which was left to him by his father. Gwen was given a settlement when she married. She had no claim to Newcombe Court except in the event of there being no surviving direct descendents of Thomas Newcombe."

"Mr. Carter, one more thing. The name Mack came up in connection with Polly—and with yourself."

"Ah, yes. Mack." Carter stared for a full minute at the limp cigar between his fingers. "Polly ran around with that fellow for a while. Mack Simmons was trouble with a capital *T*."

"What happened to him?"

"Had to get rid of him." The solicitor clamped small feral teeth around his cigar. "Oh, not like that," he said, catching Rex's expression of surprise.

"You mean, not like Tom Newcombe, who also disappeared under mysterious circumstances?"

Carter pulled the cigar from his mouth. "Are you honestly suggesting…?" he began, then stopped, apparently unable to articulate his train of thought. "No, you've got it all wrong."

"You got rid of this Mack Simmons how?"

"Paid him off, on the promise he would leave Aston. He wanted to set up a garage in Cornwall, where his mother's family was from. Far enough away, I reasoned. And far as I know, he kept his promise not to contact Polly. A solicitor friend of mine in St. Ives said he had married a local girl."

"Is Polly aware of any of this?"

"Heavens no. Part of my agreement with him was that he wouldn't divulge his whereabouts to anyone in Aston. He was amply compensated for any sentimental feelings he professed to have had for Polly. And it's not like he went to live in Siberia. St. Ives is a lovely Cornish seaside town."

"And was Polly's mother party to this arrangement?"

"It was Victoria's idea and her money."

"This took place when?"

"He left in September. The thirteenth, to be precise."

And yet Amber had told Rex that Polly and her lover had continued to meet in secret. The maid of honor was preparing to leave with parents. "Excuse me just a sec," he told Carter and hurried back to join the Willingtons at the main entrance.

"We've been released pending possible further questions," Jocelyn Willington told him in a sardonic tone, waving her farewells to the remaining guests through the open door. "What a godawful day."

"Can I borrow your daughter briefly?"

"Oh, for goodness sake. Make it quick then. Our other two daughters are home alone with our granddaughter. We'll wait in the car."

Mr. Willington nodded goodbye and accompanied his wife down the steps, leaving the gangly blonde behind at the door buttoning a coat over her flimsy pink dress.

"Amber, I know you are Polly's best friend and you don't want to betray her confidence, but I have to know—is Mack Simmons the father of her baby?"

The girl opened her mouth to speak but apparently thought better of it. "That's not for me to say," she said primly.

"It may have a bearing on the murders. You told me she and Mack continued seeing each other behind Mrs. Newcombe's back. When did he actually leave Aston?"

"Late September? Not sure exactly. Polly and I were supposed to be clothes shopping in Derby, at least that's what she told her mother, but she went to meet Mack in Aston. This was mid-September. She called me on her mobile, hysterical. He'd packed up and left without saying goodbye. Nobody at the garage knew where he'd gone. I took the next bus back from Derby. Her eyes were all red and puffy. She swore her mum had something to do with it. Days later, she said she and Mack were still seeing each other but had to be careful. Victoria was a right snob and hated him. If you really want to know, I think Polly poisoned her mum and tried to commit suicide. And no, I don't think the baby is Timmy's even though she swears it is."

"Wouldn't Polly have told you if it wasn't his?"

Amber sniffed as if recalling a hurtful slight. "She would have... before. But after that thing with Mack, she changed. She became secretive and, well, just different. A few weeks after he was supposed to have left, she started going out with Timmy, and before you knew it, they were engaged, with a baby on the way." A knowing smirk slid across the girl's blotchy face. "Anyway, she made up with her mum, and never mentioned Mack again. It was like he never existed. Is that all you wanted to know? My parents are waiting."

"Aye, thanks." But at the last moment, he called after her. The girl turned, pink dress whirling beneath her coat. "Amber," he said again. "Forgive my impertinence, but you're in love with Dudley, are you not?" He stated this matter-of-factly, recalling the longing and greed that had consumed her face when she looked at him.

She blushed to a deep shade of crimson, conveying what Rex needed to know, and ran off with an ungainly, splay-footed gait to a waiting silver Jaguar whose engine purred on idle. She jumped in the back and the car took off, spitting gravel. Her face, a pale oval looking out of the rear window, projected a vision of hopeless, un-requited passion.

"I need to go back to Aston to do some poking around," he said returning to Carter, who had planted himself in the middle of the driveway, frowning after the departing car, which had left deep ruts in the gravel. "I've pretty much exhausted the possibilities here for the time being."

"Want me to come with you?"

"Thank you, no. I think you should stay behind and hold down the fort. I believe, as an outsider, I may get further on my own."

He told Lucas he had business in Aston-on-Trent and reassured Helen it would not take long, requesting the use of her car and the keys. When she asked to go with him, he said he needed her to be his eyes and ears at Newcombe Court. Dropping a kiss on her forehead, he said goodbye and left before she had time to ask why he was going.

REX FOLLOWED THE ROAD back to Aston-on-Trent and stopped at a newsagent's to ask for directions to the doctors' clinic that Dudley had referred to at the reception.

"Won't be anyone at the clinic today," said the girl behind the counter as he turned to leave, pocketing his change from the purchase of a pouch of tobacco, in case his willpower ran out before the end of the weekend. "It's Saturday."

"Dr. Williamitis is there," put in a female shopper behind him. "I saw his car parked outside. Is it him you want to see? There are six doctors, you know."

"I wanted to speak to Dr. Thorpe's replacement."

"Dr. Thorpe? Funny you should bring his name up. His son got married today at All Saints' Church. Here you go, duck," the woman said to the shop assistant, depositing a bottle of Robinson's Lemon Barley Water and two packets of milk chocolate digestive biscuits on the counter.

"Was Dr. Thorpe your doctor?" Rex asked the woman while her items were bagged.

"He was for a time, but that was ages ago. Never had to see him for anything serious, which is probably just as well. He was a bit progressive, like. Now, when my Terry got his duodenal ulcer two years ago ..."

Oh, Lord, spare me Terry's duodenal ulcer, Rex thought, suddenly gasping at his watch and excusing himself with all speed. Once inside the car, he followed the directions he had been given to Valerie Road off Weston and, after a false turn, finally found the single-story brick clinic—but no car in the parking lot. Getting out of his vehicle, he went to peer through the glass panel door. A note was taped to the inside notifying visitors that Dr. Williamitis was on a house call and would be back "*soon*."

With a frustrated sigh, Rex cast a forlorn eye at the official hours of surgery and at the plaque on the wall listing the doctors, among them Dr. A. Williamitis. His was the only name that sounded like a disease.

Since there was nothing for him to do until the doctor returned, he drove back to the main street and without too much trouble found a space on a side road by The Malt Shovel, where he intended to plan his next move over a quiet pint. Shrugging back into his jacket, he stepped into the pub and approached the bar, which faced the weary red décor of an L-shaped lounge, the air redolent of chips and vinegar. Beneath a low beamed ceiling, the walls presented a hodgepodge of prints and farming relics, among them a yoke and shepherd's crook, recalling the region's agricultural heritage. Two chalk boards listed the menu, but in spite of the fact it was getting on for six o'clock and he was feeling the first hunger pangs of the evening, the "Fish Pie with peas & salad" failed to tempt him, still less the "Liver, onions, mash & veg." He felt too anxious to eat with so little time to solve a triple murder. A cold fireplace stood in the far corner as sunless light filtered through the small window panes.

A burly landlord loitered by the beer taps, liquor bottles ranged on shelves behind him. "What'll you have?" he asked over a background of muted Pop Rock.

"A pint of Guinness."

"Aah-do! Been ta wedding?" interrupted a toothless old man in a flat cap perched on a neighboring barstool. He jerked his head toward the pink silk carnation in Rex's lapel.

"I have," Rex answered.

"Lovely girl, our Polly. Worked as barmaid here part-time. Ah were head gardener at Newcombe when her dad were still there."

"Really?" Rex asked, turning his full attention on him.

"His missus, now, she 'ad enough of his carryings-on—"

"Now then, Jessop, that's just gossip," the landlord remonstrated as he delivered Rex's pint. Neither he nor the old man appeared to have heard of the latest goings on at Newcombe Court. The scattering of other customers around the bar and at the booths seemed similarly uninformed, judging by the lack of animation in the place.

"I 'eard 'em many a time up at house, at it like cat and dog," the old man pursued earnestly.

"Are you saying Tom Newcombe was one for the ladies?" Rex asked. He'd heard about the drinking, but this was news.

His neighbor touched his nose knowingly. "Had an auld pair working at house."

"He means an au pair," the landlord interjected, loading clean glasses onto the overhead rack while Rex downed a draught of Guinness.

"She were from one of them countries in Eastern Europe wot keep changing names," the old man went on. "Took care of his dooghter for two years, then the missus sent her packing. This were a year 'fore 'ee disappeared. Polly were nine by then."

Rex bought the old man another pint of bitter and paid for his own drink.

"Hold up, old cock," Jessop said as Rex got up to leave. "I keep a picture of the family at that time 'cause it shows the new garden."

"You still have it?"

"I can nip 'round ta m' cottage and get it."

Rex sat back down.

"He's leading you down the garden path," the landlord warned when Jessop departed in surprisingly spry fashion. "He's got nothing better to do than sit in here all day hoping people will pay for his nonsense with beer."

"But he did work for the family at the time Tom Newcombe disappeared?"

"He did, and he put the new landscaping in, what you see now." The landlord went to attend to new customers, a couple of hikers in anoraks and muddy walking boots.

Presently, Jessop returned with a colorful photo in a cheap wood frame, showing the Newcombe family and an unfamiliar young woman holding Polly by the hand. Rex scrutinized it with interest. Mother and child were instantly recognizable. Mrs. Newcombe, in a large-brimmed straw hat, smiled her superior smile.

144

Polly, pink ribbons in her pigtails, grinned out of the picture, advertising a missing front tooth.

Tom Newcombe proved a letdown, quite ordinary in every way, a man settling into the gray and slack-featured anonymity of middle age, the sort of person you passed on the street without registering any lasting impression.

"Married 'im for his money," Jessop said slyly, following Rex's facial reactions.

"Is this the au pair?" Rex pointed to the young blonde squinting at the camera.

Jessop nodded and stuck his nose back in his ale. "Belter garden, in't it?"

Rex discerned a compliment was in order. "Verra nice," he agreed, recognizing the herbaceous borders of crimson roses and lavender against a backdrop of delphiniums in dusky pink, purple and blue, still growing at Newcombe Court.

"Warn't before. It were a mess of tangled bushes and briars. We 'ad to dig it all up and put new grass down. The missus complained 'bout th' mess, but she were pleased in th' end. Even more pleased when her old man disappeared. Warn't long before that solicitor—"

"Jessop!" the landlord exploded. "That evil tongue will be the death of you."

The old man wheezed. "I knows wot I sees. If the police had asked me, I'd have told 'em to dig..."

At this point the landlord flicked his bar rag over his shoulder, pushed back the flap in the counter, and squeezing through, lifted the old man—stool, pint and all—and deposited him outside the pub entrance while Rex watched through the window. Returning,

145

he brusquely swiped his palms together. "He won't be back before tomorrow with his idle chatter. This is a warning. Next time his head gets shoved down the well for slandering the good folk from round here."

Interesting slander, nonetheless. Rex requested the local phone book from the landlord and made a note of the doctors' phone numbers from the clinic in case the aptly named Dr. Williamitis did not return from his house call in time.

In the absence of further information regarding Tom New-combe, he was left with Dr. Thorpe as a chief line of inquiry. Hopefully that would lead somewhere. An investigation comprised a confusion of false starts and dead ends, Rex often thought; but eventually, if one persevered, the right path led out of the maze.

THE CLINIC

REX WAS HUGELY RELIEVED to find a car parked outside the clinic and a stooped man carrying a doctor's bag getting out of the driver side. A pro-life sticker on the bumper imparted an element of individuality to the otherwise nondescript compact vehicle.

"Dr. Williamitis?" he called out, exiting his own car.

The man turned around. Not past forty, Rex judged by his youthful face, though his hair appeared uniformly gray and he carried his taller than average height as though bearing the weight of the world on his lean shoulders.

"Yes. Can I help you?"

"I was here earlier and saw your note. I came back hoping to speak with you."

"Are you ill?"

Just terminally curious, Rex said to himself. "I have some questions regarding Dr. Thorpe."

"Well, you had better come in out of the rain." The doctor unlocked the front door to the clinic and switched on the light in the reception area. "Come on through."

He opened an interior door to an office and gestured to a plastic bucket seat. Rex arranged himself in it while the doctor took off his raincoat and hung it from a hook on the back of the door. He lowered himself into a swivel chair behind a desk piled six inches high with files stacked around an open laptop. "Excuse the mess, but I've been updating my records."

Rex pulled one of his business cards from his wallet and half rose from his chair to place it on the desk, taking one of the doctor's as he did so. He informed Williamitis he had been aiding the Derbyshire Constabulary in the investigation of suspected murder at Newcombe Court.

The doctor slid a pair of reading spectacles up his nose and read the card. "You're from Edinburgh, I see. Naturally I could tell by your accent," he trailed off, regarding Rex quizzically above the tortoiseshell frames.

"I happened to be attending the wedding reception and alerted the police to the possibility of arsenic poisoning, having prosecuted such a case in court. The tox screen confirmed arsenic trioxide."

The doctor nodded. "One of my colleagues called me from the hospital. Do you know who ... No? Too soon, I suppose. Polly Newcombe was under Dr. Ewen's care. I hope you get to the bottom of it."

"I heard the baby was safely, though prematurely, delivered."

"By a month. Polly's due date was late June. Dr. Ewen did not elaborate on the condition of the baby or the mother."

Rex spied a file labeled *Thorpe, D.* among the stacks on the doctor's desk. "Speaking in general terms, is it possible to determine how long someone has been subjected to arsenic poisoning?"

"You are talking about chronic poisoning?"

"Aye, over a period of weeks or months."

"Arsenic builds up in the hair, skin, and nails. Exhumations have been performed to confirm the presence of arsenic in the body long after death."

"You wouldn't happen to be Timothy Thorpe's GP, would you?"

"Ye-es," the doctor said warily. "But I haven't seen him in months."

"Apparently he's been having some gastric complaints these past weeks."

"Probably just a case of wedding nerves. Oh, you're thinking it might be arsenic poisoning? Good Lord!"

"Are his brother and two children your patients also?"

Dr. Williamitis winced at the mention of Dudley Thorpe and his boys. He pulled off his glasses and wearily massaged the bridge of his nose.

"I take it you know them well," Rex prodded.

"I see them practically every week. Sometimes *twice* a week."

"Sickly kids?"

"The usual childhood ailments, and cuts and bruises you'd expect from two run-and-tumble boys of their age. But Donna Thorpe, no doubt encouraged by her mother-in-law, calls me about the slightest thing."

"Mabel Thorpe is a bit of a fussbody," Rex allowed. "I've seen how she is with Timmy."

"I was just over at Donna's. The boys have the flu and Donna complained the medicine wasn't working. Flu must run its course, I told her, but those two are hyperactive, and poor Donna looks all in. And her husband, Dudley, isn't much use. Studley," the doctor said with a wicked grin that transformed his face into a semblance of handsomeness. "Sorry, but that's my nickname for him."

Rex gave a pleased laugh. "It's a good one."

"Look, I made some coffee before I was called out. Would you like some?"

"Please," Rex said, taking in the small confines of the office with his peripheral vision and encountering no coffee machine, which meant the doctor would have to leave him unobserved for a few minutes. When Williamitis stepped outside the door, Rex visually scanned the bindings of the files while listening out for signs of the doctor's whereabouts in the small building.

"Milk, sugar?" Williamitis suddenly called out from a muffled distance.

Rex poked his head round the door. The doctor was occupied behind the glass partition of the reception desk. "Both, thanks," he called back. Then, pulling out the Thorpe file, he consigned the home address and emergency contact information to memory.

The file belonged to Dudley, Jr., judging by the birth date of the patient. The handwritten pages recording prescriptions and doctor's comments were almost illegible, but Rex was able to decipher the date when the first measles, mumps, and rubella vaccine was administered, along with a notation, "*risk of complications from mumps, viz. TPT.*" He just had time to read a scribbled recommendation for Ritalin at the appropriate age before he heard steps approaching down the short corridor.

Hurriedly, he replaced the file and assumed a relaxed pose in his uncomfortable chair.

"There you go," the doctor said handing him a mug of steaming coffee. "The National Health doesn't run to providing a good coffee machine, but the village committee pitched in and donated one. Aston-on-Trent is very community spirited. We have an annual Well Dressing Festival coming up, which draws hundreds of visitors."

Was this the well the landlord was threatening to duck Jessop into? Rex wondered. Dr. Williamitis shuffled papers on his desk while describing some of the themes of past tableaux, including the World Cup. He wore no wedding ring. Perhaps that explained why he was working on a Saturday and was happy to sit in his office and chat.

"This is a sizeable community," Rex acknowledged. "And yet it still feels like a village. Everybody seems to know everybody else."

"Well, the longer established residents do. There are close to two thousand residents now and, proportionally, more doctors. You asked about Dr. Thorpe."

"Aye. Did you know him?" Rex casually sipped his coffee, hoping for some valuable nugget out of the conversation. Such luck that he had stumbled upon the Thorpe family doctor, he reflected.

"We overlapped briefly. Sadly, he died of leukemia. He worked as long as he could in spite of the fatigue. His wife helped file his medical records, which, I must say, he kept up meticulously right to the end. We're in the process of going over to a computerized system. No help to me, unfortunately, as I find I can write faster than I can type."

No lay person could possibly transcribe the doctor's all but encrypted hieroglyphics with any degree of accuracy, Rex thought. No wonder he was entering the data himself.

"Did Dr. Thorpe treat his own family?"

"Yes, and I inherited the lot—and the hypochondria that goes with it. Not that it was all phantom diseases. His son Timmy had a severe bout of mumps when he was an adolescent. Then he developed chronic cystic acne. Poor boy had no luck, and now this. He finally finds a girl and—" The doctor trailed off into a mumble.

"Loses her?"

"I pray not."

"You and me both. Especially as she is the mother of his child."

"Yes." The doctor frowned in puzzlement at the files on his desk and murmured, "Hm."

Rex, after waiting a moment in vain for further comment, found a space on the desk and set down his empty mug. "Well, doctor, I appreciate your time and the coffee." He didn't want to outstay his welcome and he had another place to be while he still had the opportunity.

"Sorry I couldn't be of more help," Dr. Williamitis said. "Doctor-patient confidentiality and all that."

Rex thought he had been extremely helpful, but didn't want to cause the doctor any professional misgivings by saying so. They cordially shook hands, Williamitis wishing him the best with his case. "Rather a tricky proposition finding out whodunit at a wedding," he remarked, showing Rex out of the building. "Loads of suspects and strong family feeling, good and bad. I'll be following the story with keen interest, as will all of Aston, no doubt."

Rex regained his car and from the clinic retraced the road to a side street he remembered passing on the way. Blessed with a near-photographic memory, he had memorized the address in the file. Perhaps Donna could provide more details about the Thorpe and Newcombe families that might assist in the case, and the ideal time would be when Dudley was not there.

DONNA THORPE LIVED ON a street of modest detached brick homes, several of which had their curtains drawn tight against the evening gloom. As Rex looked for the right house number, he tried but failed to come up with a plausible excuse to give Dudley's wife as to why he was there.

He located the number and parked the car. Lights pouring from the downstairs window revealed tricycles and Tonka dump trucks strewn across the fenced-in square of lawn. He hoped against hope he wouldn't be interrupting the children's bath time or supper, in which case he was bound to get short shrift from the harried mother. Still, it was now or never.

Smoothing his jacket, he followed the concrete driveway to a single-car garage built three-quarters into the home, the right angle accommodating a sloping black shingle porch over a white front door with a plain glass sidelight and cheap brass letterbox. The bell resounded with a tinny ring, competing inside with a duo of shrill voices and the blare of a television. The door flew open and a young woman confronted him. She stood about five-foot-nine in her socks and on her hips carried a few pounds of excess weight that a loose-fitting sweatshirt failed to completely disguise.

"What do you want?" she demanded, the premature lines on her forehead marring an otherwise attractive face bare of makeup beneath blond-streaked hair scrunched up in a topknot.

"I take it this is not a good time, Mrs. Thorpe," Rex apologized, poised to leave.

"Depends," she said. "You been to the wedding?" She eyed his carnation and suit. "Is Dud still at Newcombe Court?"

"Aye." Looking studley and dapper in his dove gray three-piece.

As though reading his thoughts, she asked, "Chasing skirt, is he?"

Rex was spared an answer when two miniature skinheads in camouflage pajamas sprang from a door in the hall and conducted an assault on their mother's black leggings, each tugging at a limb. "Lady Madonna," sang the Beatles in his head. The boys grinned up at him, milk teeth protruding from gums surrounded by purple-smeared lips, both flushed with fever or else rabid excitement. The youngest, Rex noted, was in dire need of a nose wipe.

His heart went out to the stern-faced young mother. "Did your husband not call you that he might be late?"

"Why would he? He hardly ever calls even when he's on the road."

"Something happened at Newcombe Court. A few things, actually."

"And you are?"

"A friend of a friend of the family."

Donna shooed the boys back into the room whence the TV emitted a cacophony of American cartoon voices. "Come in," she said. Standing to one side so Rex could pass into the narrow hall, she mechanically asked if her husband was okay. A smell of toast, baked beans and soured talcum powder wafted in the warm air circulating from the central heating.

"He's fine," Rex told her, "but I'm sorry to say that Victoria Newcombe died from arsenic poisoning today."

Donna stared at him in incredulity as, slowly, her hands went to her face. She wore a flashy engagement ring, vastly at odds with her attire and the black nail polish half worn away above the cuticles. "She's dead?"

"I'm afraid so. Polly was poisoned too. They delivered her child by emergency C-section this afternoon."

"Arsenic." Donna turned and clasped the white-painted banister leading up the steep stairs. The finish on the walls, of the same flat white, like primer, contributed to the flimsy look of the house.

"Do you know the Newcombes well?" he inquired gently.

"I haven't seen Polly in ages. How's Timmy?"

"Seems okay. However, I've just come from the clinic, and Timmy has not been in to see Dr. Williamitis in months, which is odd considering he's been feeling a bit off lately, by all accounts."

"His mum likes to tell him what's good for him. And anyway, Timmy avoids waiting rooms like the plague, afraid he'll pick up germs, and rarely comes to our house in case he catches something off the kids. So, the baby's okay?"

"Hopefully. Were you surprised when you found out aboot Timmy's and Polly's baby?"

"What do you mean? What's it got to do with me?"

156

"I heard it happened a bit fast, you know with the engagement and everything."

"The same thing happened with us. I fell pregnant, we got married, and before we knew it, another was on the way. Dud wasn't keen for me to go to his brother's wedding. My mom could've taken care of the boys. I had a dress picked out and everything, but he wasn't having any of it."

"Has your husband ever mentioned Bobby Carter?"

"That's the solicitor, isn't it? Dud swears he and Mrs. Newcombe have been having it off for years. Well, she's dead now, you said. Why—"

Just then, an earsplitting shriek erupted from the living room. Rex wondered about the wisdom of leaving two little thugs to their own devices. "Maaaa," bawled one.

"Should I check on the lads? Sounds like Armageddon has broken out."

"The room is child-proofed," Donna said in a monotone, but she went in anyway and yelled at them to settle down. The threat of early bedtime successfully meeting with instantaneous silence, she closed the door on them.

"A handful?"

"Brendan is two and Duddie three. What do you expect?"

"I have a lad of my own."

"Still living at home?"

"No, he's away at university in Florida."

"Florida?" Donna's face assumed a wistful look. "I used to dream about going to America. I did some modeling in my teens. I know; hard to believe, looking at me now." She glanced despairingly at the multi-stained yellow sweatshirt bagging over her black leggings. She gave the impression of a wasp, though Rex felt sure it wasn't intentional. "I didn't even have time to shower this morning. God, I must look a sight."

"It'll get easier."

"When?" she pleaded, gazing up into his face before slumping onto the bottom step of the stairs, decked in a garish green print continuing the wall-to-wall carpeting in the hall.

Hysterical giggles escaped from the front room. Seconds later, the door creaked open and two cheeky smirks appeared in the aperture.

Rex went in and, scooping one squirming tot in each arm, lifted them over the backrest of the sofa and plunked them down on the black faux leather in front of the flat screen TV. Looming over them, he pointed a finger at each sticky and terror-stricken face. "Now, do *not* move until I tell you."

Exiting the room, he left the door ajar and returned to the exhausted mother. "Want to tell me aboot it, lass?" Something was troubling her. Was it just the fact of being stuck at home with two rambunctious kids? Somehow, he felt something more was afoot.

Donna, forehead reposing in her lap, clasped her knees and rocked back and forth on the stairs. "I feel like a prisoner," she moaned. "I daren't go out of the house. Everything's in hock. The telly will be next. They've started calling the house!"

"Who is calling the house?"

"The people Dud owes money to. Listen to this." She jumped to her feet and lifted the phone bodily from the hall table, unraveling the line as she returned to the stairs. She set it on her knees and lifted the handset. "I saved this message," she told Rex, pressing a button.

158

He sat beside her on the step, their thighs touching in the confined space.

"We know where to find you, Mr. Dudley," a male voice intoned from the receiver. *Click*.

"That's it?" Rex asked.

"I didn't save the others. What d'you think?"

"It sounds a wee bit sinister. Have you called the police?"

Donna shook her head, causing her topknot to slip from its yellow band. "Dud won't hear of it. He's waiting on his commissions from the sale of his hot tubs. He says he can pay these scum off."

"Who are they? And why did the man on the phone call him Mr. Dudley and not Mr. Thorpe?"

Donna shrugged. "You see, Dud bets on the horses."

"Ah."

"He promised he'd stop. But he won't, not until they break his knee caps. That's what they threatened on the last message." She looked at Rex. "When you rang the bell, I thought at first you might be one of them. But you sounded different, and you seem like a gentleman. Even if you had been one of Dud's creditors, I wouldn't have cared. It's almost worse not knowing what's going to happen, what they'll repossess next. My car's gone. I know how Dud's going to get out of this mess. I only hope he did it to protect me and the boys, and not just to save his own precious skin."

"Are you suggesting he perpetrated a crime to pay off his debts?" Rex asked, mindful of her reaction to Victoria Newcombe's death.

"He poisoned Mrs. Newcombe and her daughter, didn't he? That's what you came to tell me. So Timmy would inherit Newcombe Court. Dud could always twist Timmy around his little finger and get money off him."

159

"Mrs. Thorpe, Dudley has not been charged with anything. Suspicion is more likely to attach to someone who was at Newcombe Court early this morning."

"Dud wasn't with me all morning. He went out to see a man about some business, or so he said."

"How long was he gone?"

"An hour, hour and a half. When he got back, he took a shower, got all dressed up, and left me here with the kids, waiting for the doctor."

"The police will want to confirm everyone's alibis in due course."

"Did Dud send you to explain why he was held up?"

Rex wished he could answer in the affirmative. "No, I came under my own steam. The detective in charge is letting me follow an independent line of investigation, providing I demonstrate the utmost discretion." At least, Lucas hadn't told him not to.

"Why would he let you do that?"

"I undertake private cases on occasion."

"You're from Edinburgh, aren't you? I always liked a refined Scots burr."

"My name is Rex Graves." He rummaged in his wallet for a business card. "I should have introduced myself sooner."

She smiled weakly and stared in deep thought at the phone. Since she made no attempt to take the card, he left it on the stairs. Bumping and squelching sounds from the leather sofa in the other room punctuated a round of animated character voices on the TV.

"I can get my mum to watch the kids for a bit," Donna decided, picking up the receiver. "I want to go round to Mabel's, do a bit of digging into Dud's finances. He keeps all that stuff there. I'd feel safer if you came with me. Can you?"

Tugging back his cuff, Rex glanced at his watch: 7:30. "I don't know if Mabel will be back home yet. She and Timmy went to the hospital and are supposed to return to Newcombe Court."

"There's a spare key she keeps on the window ledge. Dud sometimes uses it. I just need the recent bank statements, to see how much is in the account. All his private papers and financial documents are at his old home. Timmy helps with his taxes."

"What would Mabel say if you went in her house when she wasn't home?"

"What could she say? If Dud is hiding stuff from me, I've a right to know."

"Might be better if you waited until she got back."

"She won't let me look in his old room. She always takes his side. It's not like I'm going to take anything—I just want to look. I'll say I forgot Duddie's toy gun and he was screaming for it." She started dialing. "But in case someone's after Dud and I'm followed, I need you to come with me."

Rex hesitated, loath to become embroiled in the domestic dispute.

"It won't take long. It's less than a kilometer away."

Seeing the despair in her eyes, he nodded in confirmation. He could not let her go alone and, in any event, he welcomed the excuse to see the Thorpe family home. He rose from the stairs and, returning to the front room, found Duddie in the process of smothering his younger brother with a sofa cushion. When he saw Rex, he shot back into a sitting position. Brendan, curled into a ball, pummeled the cushion with his feet. When he, too, caught sight of Rex, he froze and stared up at him with masochistic delight.

161

Rex pulled a clean handkerchief from his pocket and, bending down, wiped the boy's nose for him, removing what he could of the encrusted gunk surrounding it with deft swoops of the linen. A sippy cup containing what looked like Ribena had come unscrewed and was leaking black currant juice onto the cream rug. He attempted to mop that up too, but it soaked into his handkerchief, forcing him to abandon it on the floor rather than risk staining the lining of his pocket. He rose wearily to his feet.

"Your gran might be coming to watch you both for a while," he informed the boys. "Your mum's mum," he specified so they knew which one.

"Nan, Nan, Nan," the eldest started chanting, enthusiastically joined by his brother in a piping falsetto as he bounced up and down on the sofa.

Donna appeared and admonished the kids. "Their nan lives around the corner," she told Rex. "I'll get my shoes. Can we go in your car?"

"No problem." He followed her back into the hall, still a tad hesitant about what he was getting into.

"I tried Dud on his mobile but he's not answering, so I called Timmy. The baby is in intensive care and Polly is still out of it. He's heading back to Newcombe with his mum."

At that moment, an older and thicker Donna let herself in the front door, her surprised glance roving over the strange man in her daughter's hallway. With one hand, she unknotted her headscarf beaded with raindrops and, pulling it off, draped it over the wooden coat tree in the corner. She wore an array of Zircon studs in her left ear beneath an upsweep of bleached blond hair cut short at the back.

"I've brought the fairy cakes I made with the boys this morning," she told Donna, holding up a plastic container.

"Nan, Nan!" a crescendo of voices spilled from the front room.

"Coming," the elder woman responded, upbeat and in control, much like a general about to enter the fray.

"Best take your plastic poncho," she advised her daughter. "It's coming down heavy." She stared in concern at Donna's face. "You going to tell me what's going on?"

"When I get back," Donna promised. "But something bad has happened. Mr. Graves is here to help. He's a private detective."

"Listen, Donna," Rex cautioned. "May I call you Donna? I may not be helping you at all. If your husband is involved in the Newcombe business, I need to know."

"What Newcombe business?" Donna's mother asked. "Is it about money?" Clearly she did not have any close friends among the Newcombes or Thorpes who might have called her with news of the murders. Rex decided this wasn't the time to enlighten her. He and Donna had to get going.

"In the unlikely event Dud calls, I'm in the shower," Donna instructed, grabbing a transparent poncho from the coat tree and opening the front door. "Don't worry," she added.

Her mother looked no less worried at hearing this.

Rex passed in front of her. "Wait here while I pull up the car." Turning up the collar of his jacket, he plunged headlong into the rain.

"Take care of her, Mr. Graves," Donna's mother called after him.

163

Donna directed Rex to Mabel's house, having spent the brief drive looking over her shoulder and airing her anxieties about the hit men who were threatening her husband. "I just don't know what they'll stop at," she said more than once. "If they've got our home phone number, they know our address, as we're listed."

This was not at all reassuring to Rex, who was fond of his knee caps. "What will you do with the information you find?" he asked, unpersuaded that Donna had thought this through logically, as was often the case with people under considerable stress.

"I'll consider my options."

"Your mother seems a together sort of person," he offered as consolation.

"She's a godsend, but she hasn't any money to help us. She warned me against marrying Dud. Stop! It's this one right here."

Rex parked on the street in front of the white end-of-terrace house Donna had indicated. The windows, hung with net curtains, were unlit from within. A dim globe light beneath the stone porch roof revealed a glass-paned door. His phone stirred in his jacket. Drawing it from his pocket, he saw Helen's name on the display. Oops. He'd been gone longer than intended.

"Rex! Where are you?"

"I'm still in Aston chasing down leads. What's going on at Newcombe Court?"

"The police are still here dithering about."

"Are the Thorpes there?"

"Yes, all three. When are you coming back?"

"Verra soon, lass, I promise." He snapped his phone shut and returned it to his pocket.

"Was that your wife?" Donna asked.

"My fiancée. A truly understanding woman. Ready?"

She nodded but seemed reluctant to leave the peace and warmth of the car. He was anxious to take a quick look inside the house before Mabel got home. Even if Donna had a flimsy pretext for being there, he had none.

"I hope you get on well with your mother-in-law," he said.

"She interferes a lot and, of course, no one is good enough for her Dudley." Donna sat looking at her hands, her diamond solitaire sparkling with white fire in the gloom. "Dud wanted me to pawn it," she said, holding up the fingers of her left hand. "But I won't."

On that note, she opened the passenger door. The rain had eased off again. Avoiding the puddles, Rex followed her up the path to the porch.

"Oh, bugger, it's not here," Donna said sweeping her fingers along the window ledge. "It's usually kept in a crack at this end. What are we going to do?"

Heck if I know, Rex thought. This was, to be sure, an anticlimactic turn of events. "Why does Mabel keep a spare key outside?"

"Timmy is forgetful."

"That's true," Rex said, recalling the scene at the church gate when Mabel had reminded her son about his inhaler and Tums. Rex looked around for another suitable hiding place for the key. "He's also quite tall," he murmured, reaching into a hanging basket of purple and yellow pansies above his head.

People were often more concerned about accidentally being locked out of their homes than about a burglar finding an easy way in, as he had learned from trying cases of home invasion. Feeling uncomfortably like a burglar himself, he groped among the velvety petals and discovered the small hard item he sought.

"*Eureka*," he said, holding up the key.

Donna grabbed it and rammed it into the keyhole. "I bet they put it up there so I wouldn't find it."

The door opened. Rex took the key and replaced it in the basket.

Once inside, Donna threw off her wet poncho. Before either of them could make another move, a thud from behind the door to their right froze them to the spot. Rex's heart leaped to his throat. Seemed they weren't alone after all. By the porch light seeping through the frosted glass, Rex signaled for them to get out. That's when he heard a *meow*.

Donna put a restraining hand on his sleeve. "It's only Monty." As she switched on the light in the stairwell, a large ginger tom tore out of the room and bolted for the back of the house, tail at half mast.

"I would have thought Timmy was the type to be allergic to cats."

"He's not, but Dud is. Timmy's had him eight years." Donna mounted the stairs. "I'm going to check out my husband's old room. Keep watch, will you? Best lock the door."

Rex did so and followed the ginger tom's path to the kitchen. Donna must have put the light on in Dudley's room. An upstairs window shed illumination on the walled-in garden, which backed onto those of a similar row of terraced homes. He decided to risk putting on the kitchen light since the house was already lit up like Vegas.

The orange tom, a shorthaired species with a white chin and snowy forepaws, stood by the cat flap eying him, waiting perhaps to see if the stranger would replenish his food bowl. Rex had not expected to find anything as companionable and homely as this fine fellow at Mabel's abode, for she had struck him as somewhat sterile and austere. When Monty saw that no treats were forthcoming, he head-butted the flap, and his furry hindquarters and striped tail followed through the gap, leaving Rex alone.

The kitchen, though not ultra-modern, was neat and orderly. Two cups and saucers had been left upside down to dry on the draining board. Ditto a pair of teaspoons. A quick and careful look in the dishwasher revealed two neatly stacked breakfast bowls and plates, as yet unwashed. His gaze rested on the blue tin canisters on the Formica counter by the stove, labeled Tea, Coffee, and Sugar, but he refrained from rifling through the cabinets. An in-depth search was well outside his purview, and he was on extremely thin ice being here in the first place. He wished Donna would hurry up. He had an uncomfortable feeling about the whole situation.

His shoes squeaked on the shiny linoleum as he tiptoed into the dinette, where half the table was spread with bills and correspondence. A Welsh dresser in dark mahogany, matching the table, displayed a crockery set of the same blue floral design as the tea cups by the sink and the bowls and plates in the dishwasher—serviceable ware but not fine china, in keeping with what he had seen so far of the house. On a shelf mainly reserved for cookery books, his eye picked out a number of medical encyclopedias and books on accounting.

A creak sounded on the landing upstairs. Rex flipped off the kitchen light and returned to the hall, glancing into the shadowy living room as he passed and confirming his impression of a functional and comfortable house, but not one on which a lot of money had been lavished. Perhaps Mabel had downgraded after Dr. Thorpe's death.

"Find what you were looking for?" he called up the stairs.

Receiving no answer, he climbed the carpeted steps two at a time and, taking a right turn on the landing, entered the room directly above the kitchen. No Donna.

A brown shag pile rug curled up against the base boards. In a corner perpendicular to the window lay a narrow bed draped with a beige crochet coverlet. Continuing anticlockwise, his gaze took in a bedside table and a small desk beneath the window ledge, each with the drawers hanging open and, against the third wall, a wardrobe whose doors stood agape, empty but for a few boxes on the upper shelf.

Across from the desk, a cheap set of shelves sagged beneath a boyhood collection of old textbooks, sports trophies, and souvenirs from the seaside—shells, artfully shaped driftwood, and colored bottles washed up on some shore. Posters of soccer stars tacked to the patterned wallpaper and a crossbow propped in a corner behind the door lent an element of masculinity to the old-maidish décor and rounded out his inventory of the most noteworthy items in the room.

Donna wandered through the doorway, holding a depleted checkbook and a sheaf of bank statements. "Couldn't find anything next door," she informed him. "I didn't dare touch Timmy's stuff as he'd notice if anything was out of place. This is what I found in here."

She brandished the contents in her hand. "We're still in the black, but only just. Twenty-eight quid in the chequing account to last us until the end of the month. Nothing in savings. I found several large cash withdrawals, which would be for his bookie. And something else. A cancelled cheque to a Doctor Forspaniak for almost the amount of our monthly mortgage, dated November of last year. Dud's never been ill in his life, except for the occasional hangover."

"Maybe it was supplemental care for his mother."

"Mabel has the constitution of an ox, though you wouldn't think it to look at her. Timmy bears the brunt of ailments in that family."

"Let's get everything put back the way it was," Rex suggested, keen to get going now that Donna had what she'd come for and he'd gained an insight into the Thorpe family home.

As they moved toward the door, Rex cocked a thumb in the direction of the wooden bow. "Does your husband fancy himself as Robin Hood?"

Donna snortled. "You mean rob the rich to give to the poor? Meaning himself. Yeah, maybe."

"You seriously think he poisoned the Newcombe family to get hold of their money?"

"Don't you? That's why you came to see me, isn't it? He could easily have gone to Newcombe Court this morning. Besides, he had access to the arsenic."

"Did he?"

"Well, he'd know where to get hold of some. His dad used it to treat his leukemia."

"What?" Rex asked in astonishment.

"It didn't work, but it's in one of the medical books about cures for cancer downstairs."

Rex had no more time to assimilate this information. A scuffling noise at the front door arrested Donna in the process of switching off the light to Dudley's room. From the landing, Rex glimpsed a large shadow behind the door pane. A key turned in the lock.

Donna yanked Rex into an airing cupboard at the top of the stairs and swiftly drew the louver doors closed. It felt warm and cramped in the closet, claustrophobically so, and he had to keep his head bowed. Had Mabel returned, her form magnified through the opaque glass in the door? What would she think if she found her daughter-in-law and the Scotsman from the reception hiding in her cupboard? A sharp scent of lavender laundry detergent pricked at his nostrils and he feared he might sneeze. Wrangling an arm free in the limited space, he pressed his hand to his nose. Donna stiffened beside him as footsteps stomped up the creaking stairs.

Perspiration began to pool in the armpits of his jacket. Between the slats of the doors, he made out the back of a broad figure in a dark hooded jacket. The individual paused on the landing, darting his head in both directions, and then pushed open the door to Dudley's room. The light went on, the door closed. Nudging Donna, Rex eased open the louver doors and led her down the inside tread of the stairs to avoid creaking boards, while the scrape and juddering of displaced furniture on bare floor continued above them.

In the hall, Rex tripped over the plastic poncho Donna had dropped on their way in and held out an arm to brace himself, hitting the door as he did so. They exchanged a panicked look.

Rex stopped her as she bent to retrieve the garment. Turning back the knob on the front door, he shot a look up the stairs. All clear. He gently clicked the door shut after them. Then, grabbing Donna by the arm, he dragged her across the grass beside the boundary hedge and through a gap to the car. Helen's car beeped as he hit the remote, but it couldn't be helped. Dudley's room, in any case, was on the far side of the house. However, on the off chance he'd been heard, he started the engine and pulled out without lights, not wishing to be seen. At the end of the street, Donna broke the silence.

"Did you see who it was?"

"A man with large shoulders wearing a hoodie."

"Dud doesn't have a hoodie."

That you know of, thought Rex. It appeared there were other things about which Dudley kept Donna in the dark. He sped up, lights now on full beam in the rain, and headed down the deserted road toward her house. "If that wasn't your husband, how did he know which room to look in?" he asked.

"Why would Dud ransack his own room? I hope it's not him. He'd recognize my poncho and give me grief for sneaking into his mom's house. I don't know what Mabel is going to say when she finds it. You should've let me take it."

"It was as squeaky as a wet balloon. And whoever it was must have seen it and would have noticed if it was gone. Best tell Mabel you went over and someone else was there. In fact, call the police right now." He handed Donna his phone.

He regretted not having apprehended the intruder himself, but he had no idea whom he was dealing with, in addition to which his own presence was a bit sticky to explain.

"Dud would kill me if I called the police."

"What if your mother-in-law's house is being burgled?"

"There's nothing worth stealing at Mabel's. And it wasn't a break-in. The person used a key."

"So did we. Perhaps he was watching us."

"Look, I'll call her when I get home, okay?" Donna returned his phone and he dropped it into his pocket with a sigh of resignation and a feeling that events were spiraling out of control.

"Okay, but make sure you do. And tell the police about the threatening phone calls while you're at it. Things have a way of escalating where loan sharks are involved."

"Dud should be able to fob them off now that he's related to the Newcombe family, especially with Victoria out of the way. But if he goes to prison for murder, they might come after me for what he owes." She bit her lip and gazed numbly out the window.

Donna had a point, Rex conceded. She was a brave lass and she had brains, but would prove no match for a gang of vicious hoodlums. The car slushed to a stop outside her home and the front door flew open. Silhouetted in the doorway, Donna's mother threw them a friendly wave, in which no small measure of relief was apparent.

"Will you call me when you find out anything?" Donna asked.

"Of course. Now take your two lads and stay at your mother's house tonight, just to be safe. And call Mabel immediately."

He waited to drive off until she was securely inside, hoping she would heed his advice. A lot of strange events were taking place, and even he didn't feel safe.

WHEN REX HAD SET out for Aston-on-Trent in the search for answers, he had not anticipated running into thugs who were capable of resorting to bodily harm as a means of persuasion. However, as well as taking an unexpected turn, his investigation had turned up a few interesting leads. On the drive back to Newcombe Court, he called Dr. Williamitis at the clinic. The doctor picked up on the first ring.

"It's Rex Graves calling. I had a couple more questions aboot Dr. Thorpe, if you have time."

"Go ahead."

"Is arsenic trioxide used as a cure for leukemia?"

"Under the trade name Trisenox, it's sometimes used in cases where the leukemia is unresponsive to first line agents." Rex strained to hear over the noise of the engine and passing cars. "But due to the toxic nature of arsenic, Trisenox, which works partly by killing cancer cells, also carries significant risks. In Dr. Thorpe's case, the drug caused acute promyelocytic leukemia differentiation syndrome, which ultimately proved fatal."

"How was the drug administered?"

"Intravenously, at home," Williamitis stated. "You had another question?"

Clearly, this was the end of the discussion on Dr. Thorpe's battle with cancer.

"I'm wondering if you might have heard of a Dr. Forspaniak?"

This time a marked pause ensued. "Yes," said the doctor, drawing out the word with obvious reluctance. "I know a Dr. Forspaniak. Not sure if it's the same person you're enquiring about."

"Well, tell me about the one you know."

"He's a gynecologist with a practice in Derby. He also performs abortions. In extreme cases, I refer patients to him."

After thanking the doctor for his help, Rex pressed his foot on the gas, anxious to reach Newcombe Court before Inspector Lucas departed.

By the time he arrived, noticeably fewer vehicles filled the driveway. Night enshrouded the park. The men in anoraks assisting with the parking earlier that day had been the bartender and carver.

"Had to let the servers and most of the guests go," the inspector told Rex, meeting him inside the front door of the great hall.

Only a handful of people remained, seated now as one group by the fireplace opposite the one from which the miniature bride and groom had been salvaged. Rex could not see Helen.

"My gut tells me Bobby Carter knows more than he's saying," Lucas said, "but we can't prove anything. He just waffles on about his attachment to the family and his failure to protect them. Crocodile tears, if you ask me. Now then, you went to Aston." Lucas put the emphasis on the word Aston, evidently demanding an explanation.

Rex filled him in on his visits with Dr. Williamitis and Donna Thorpe, sticking to the facts for now and skirting around his suspicions and suppositions. "I went to her house on spec and found out more than I anticipated."

"Donna Thorpe was our next stop," Lucas informed him. "So her husband was out this morning on some unexplained business, hmm? We'll need to talk to the bookie." He made a note in his pad. "How much is our Dudley in the hole for?"

"She doesn't know, but apparently enough to make it worth hiring some heavies to retrieve it."

"It's motive for the poisoning," the inspector surmised. "Especially if you factor in what you found out about Dr. Thorpe using arsenic to treat his leukemia. Too much of a coincidence, by half. Of course, we would need to prove that Dudley got hold of the arsenic and was able to inject it in the cake without anyone noticing him. No one saw him here this morning."

Perrin hovered expectantly.

"Well, what is it?" the inspector snapped.

"Call from the divisional commander, sir. Wants to know why you won't answer your mobile."

"Because I've got my ruddy hands full, that's why."

"He says it's important." Perrin gingerly held out a cell phone at the end of a lanky arm.

The inspector swiped it off him. "Yes, sir," he said brightly into the phone. "We are making fair progress. Sergeant Dartford is down at the station going over Jasmina Patel's and Harry Futuro's statements—" As he listened, he fidgeted in his pocket. At length, he drew out an elastic band, which he wound around the thumb of his free hand with his forefinger, pulling tight with a fixed expression of glee as though going through the motions of garroting the senior officer. Suddenly he stopped. "Really, sir? . . . I see. Romania. Yes, this case does seem to be getting bigger. No, I'm sure we can contain it."

His caller monopolized the conversation for some minutes. "I'll send Sergeant Dartford over to Worley Station right away," Lucas said. With an absent gesture, the inspector pressed the call-end button on the phone.

"Developments, sir?" Perrin asked, arms clasped respectfully behind his back as he flexed his calves in his standard issue black shoes.

"You could say that." Lucas turned to Rex. "The presumed suicide off the bridge at Worley Station has been identified as Thomas Newcombe. A preliminary examination of the body showed a perforation in the heart and a small amount of blood. We are now treating the death as suspicious."

"Thomas Newcombe, as in Victoria Newcombe's husband?" Perrin asked. Rex could tell the youth was having a field day and doubtless enjoyed the diversion from routine shifts on the beat writing up reports on acts of vandalism and public disturbance.

"The same. Seems he flew into Heathrow from Bucharest last night and got a train to Worley this morning."

"That's about twenty minutes from here, isn't it, sir?"

"That's right."

Rex stood by while Lucas got back on the phone and relayed the information to Sergeant Dartford at the police station. "He arrived at Worley at 9:15 this morning. There was a note in his briefcase. I want you to bring it to me...No, the note was addressed to him, giving instructions where to meet and signed 'M.'"

"'M' for Murder?" Perrin asked Rex in an excited aside.

"This isn't a Hitchcock movie, Perrin," Lucas sniped, and switched his attention back to the phone. "Hole consistent with a small sharp instrument. Go and see the coroner...No, cause of death looks like the fall and/or impact of the train. The briefcase contained his boarding pass stub and return flight information. He was planning to return to Romania Tuesday...No, only the briefcase; perhaps he left a bag at the hotel or wherever he stayed last night. Find out what you can." Lucas flipped the phone shut and stared meditatively at the floor.

"The plot thickens?" Rex asked the inspector with a wink at Perrin.

"The body count is certainly mounting. Vicar dead, Mrs. Newcombe dead, Polly Newcombe in limbo, the aunt dead, and now her brother turns up dead."

"On the subject of Tom Newcombe, I found out something that may have some bearing." Rex repeated the gossip he had heard at the pub relating to the dead man and the au pair from Eastern Europe. "Jessop is the old man's name. Claims to have witnessed some domestic disturbance while working here as head gardener. Not sure how reliable his information is, but the landlord at The Malt Shovel can let you know where to find him."

Inspector Lucas wrote in his notepad. "Thanks." He punctuated his gratitude by stabbing the page with his pencil. "Who've we got left here among the guests?" he asked Perrin.

The constable looked around, sparing the inspector the trouble. "The solicitor, the Thorpes, Littons, Helen d'Arcy, Meredith Matthews, and her boyfriend Reggie Cox. And the two caterers."

"Ask who knew Thomas Newcombe was on his way to the wedding today. A clipping of the announcement of his daughter's engagement was found at his home in Romania, according to my superior. Stands to reason he was back in the country to see her get married."

"Was this his first time back in England in ten years?" Rex inquired.

"Appears so. The home address on his EU driving licence is a farm in a small village outside Bucharest. The local police went to notify the residents of his death this afternoon. A woman who identified herself as his wife confirmed that he had travelled to England on business, but she didn't know much else except that he was aware of his eldest daughter's engagement. Seems she and Newcombe have a young daughter together."

The inspector delved into his pocket and pulled out his container of aspirin, which he upturned into his mouth, staring up at the remote ceiling through bloodshot eyes.

"Shall I get you some water, sir?" Perrin offered.

His superior ground down on the pills, looking as dazed and woebegone as a man waking up from a hangover. He gave the plastic bottle an inquiring shake of the contents.

How many more did the man intend to take? Rex wondered. "Perhaps some coffee," he told the constable. "It looks like it's going to be a long night."

CARTER COAXED HIS CIGAR to life through a quick succession of drawn-in breaths, seemingly unconcerned about smoking indoors, even if it was in a spacious room with a lofty ceiling. "I saved these Cuban cigars for the occasion," he said wistfully.

Rex felt for his pipe, and then stuffed it back down in his pocket. "A small sharp object, the coroner said," he recounted, expanding on the details of Tom Newcombe's death.

"The point of an umbrella? It was raining today, after all."

"Those don't have very sharp points though, do they? I was thinking more along the lines of an ice pick, such as the one the bartender was using."

"They don't search you at railway stations, so any kind of weapon would have been possible, I suppose. Hm! To think Thomas has been living in Romania all these years with the au pair. The sly old dog. Victoria would be furious." Carter took a puff and lowered his cigar. "You don't think his murder has anything to do with the deaths here, do you? Could just have been an argument

180

on the bridge, perhaps with one of his old antique dealer colleagues."

Rex shook his head doubtfully. "Seems a bit coincidental to me that we have these murders at Newcombe Court, and the owner finally turns up after ten years for his daughter's wedding, and he's murdered as well."

"Why not just feed him some wedding cake like the others?"

"Too risky. By then, people would have known whom he'd been in contact with."

"Who?"

"Therein lies the key to the whole mystery."

"Mind if I borrow him?" Helen asked Carter with a determined smile. Linking Rex's arm, she drew him to an empty sofa by the fireside. "I didn't know you were back. I was having tea with Stella Pembleton in the kitchen."

"What are Meredith and Reggie still doing here?"

"We were supposed to give them a lift back to Derby. They've missed their train to London so I said they could spend the night with us."

"Could they not have stayed with Elaine and Jeremy?"

"Their flat is too small. And, anyway, Reggie is hoping to sell his story to a tabloid. A couple of reporters have already been 'round here."

"I just don't want to keep them waiting. There have been further developments. You get on home. I can find my own way back to Derby."

Helen gave a patient sigh. "What developments?"

Rex explained about the body at Worley Station.

"The one that Reggie and Meredith were talking about on the way here?"

"Exactly. Looks like Tom Newcombe was stabbed before he took a dive off the bridge. So Inspector Lucas has reopened the round of questioning."

Helen sank back on the sofa. "This defies belief, Rex. Someone is out to kill every member of the Newcombe family. That means the first murder occurred before the poisonings and before Aunt Gwen was pushed from the tower. And doesn't that sound eerily like the way poor Mr. Newcombe died? Was he fatally stabbed or was he killed when he fell in front of the train?"

Rex felt Helen shudder and squeezed her hand. "I overheard Inspector Lucas say the fall or the train finished him off."

At that moment his phone vibrated. Pulling it out of his pocket, he saw it was a local number. "Rex Graves," he answered, wondering who the caller might be.

"It's Donna. You left your business card, so I hope you don't mind..."

"Donna? Are you okay?" Instinctively, he got up and started to pace.

"I'm in serious trouble. You've got to help me." Her words sounded strained and effortful. "I told them you would arrange to get them the money." A sob escaped into the phone. "They're threatening to take my ring and my finger with it if I don't pay up," she cried, her voice rising in panic.

"How much do they want?"

"Four thousand quid," she blurted. "That's what Dud owes."

"Are 'they' the people you mentioned earlier?"

"Yes, but I can't talk about them. I said you could get the money from Bobby Carter. He looks after the family interests and Dud is family now."

"Do you want me to bring Dudley to the phone?"

"No! They don't trust him. I said you were my lawyer and you could get them the money. Please!"

Rex waved his arm in the air and waggled his fingers, attempting to get the inspector's attention at the far end of the hall. "Get Lucas and Carter here," he mouthed to Helen. "Okay, Donna," he resumed. "But it's the weekend. How do they propose we get that amount of cash at short notice? Presumably they won't take a cheque..."

"They want a banker's draft made out to bearer delivered first thing Monday morning. They'll release me until then. If I don't get the money, they'll kidnap me again whenever they get the chance and dump me somewhere. And you can't talk to the police."

"Can I speak to your abductors?"

"They won't speak to anyone directly."

"Where are your lads?"

"At my mom's." Rex heard her blow her nose. "I was leaving my house with an overnight bag when they bundled me into a van and blindfolded me—Ow!"

"What happened?"

"One of them hit me. I'm not supposed to give away any information."

Inspector Lucas and Bobby Carter approached. Rex held them at bay with one hand and motioned for them to be quiet. Helen returned to her spot on the sofa and watched his face with rapt attention.

"Donna, I have Bobby Carter with me. Let me see what I can sort out."

Inspector Lucas, who must have received the gist of the call from Helen, gestured for the phone. "Hello, Donna, I am Robert Carter, the Newcombe family solicitor," he impersonated. "So Dudley has got himself into a spot of bother, has he?... To the tune of four grand. I see ..."

Lucas was doing his best to refine his normal voice and sound more like a solicitor than a copper. Rex only hoped the men demanding the ransom were unaware of the police presence at Newcombe Court. If they were keeping a low profile, it was possible they had not heard about the murders yet. Doubtful that Donna in her plight had felt the necessity of filling her captors in on what Rex had told her in Aston regarding the poisonings. "Well, I'm sure it won't come to that," Lucas said after listening for a moment. "Can I speak to the person in charge? ... Yes, I'll hold."

The inspector raised pale ginger eyebrows at Rex as he waited. "As if we didn't have enough to deal with," he muttered. "Any problem about raising the cash?" he asked Carter, holding the phone to his chest. The solicitor shook his head as Lucas returned the phone to his ear. "No, we're not recording the call, Donna ... How do we get the banker's draft to you? ... Yes, I'll tell him—"

The inspector turned to Rex. "She rang off. The people holding her wouldn't speak to me. She'll make contact with you Monday morning. Let's see what the incoming number is. She said she was calling from a pay phone."

He then summoned PC Perrin. He decided the constable should go round to Donna's mother's house and interview her in case she had seen or heard anything that might lead to the kidnappers, and he should then talk to the bookie. Dispersing the guests in the immediate vicinity, Lucas informed Dudley of the situation and got his mother-in-law's address off him.

Dudley leaned forward on the sofa with the heels of his palms cupping his eyeballs. "I don't believe this," he groaned.

Rex almost felt sorry for him, even though he had brought it upon himself.

REX CAUGHT UP WITH Stella Pembleton as the caterers made for the front door after being told by the inspector they were free to go. "You must be relieved to know that inorganic arsenic caused the fatal symptoms and not any negligence on your part," he told her.

"It certainly is a relief. Not sure where it leaves Pembleton Caterers, though. News of the murders will be all over the media."

"There are more sensationalistic aspects to this case than who prepared the buffet. With any luck your name won't come up."

"Do you know who did it?" Stella asked.

"We may be close. In fact, I wanted to ask you when you might have left the wedding cake unattended this morning, before you iced the top."

Stella's features drew taut as she gave the question some thought. "Oh, goodness. As I told the police, I was in and out of the kitchen. Lydia asked me to see that she had placed the flowers correctly. And then Mr. Carter couldn't find his private stash of malt whisky and got into an altercation with the bartender, which I had to referee. Victoria Newcombe was upstairs getting ready. It's stressful when people interfere with the arrangements at the last minute."

"Did Bobby Carter find his whisky?"

"Eventually. But only after all the staff went hunting for it. He must have set the bottles down at the front door when he rang the bell this morning, and then forgotten about them. But he swore he had put them on the sideboard."

"When was this?"

"Nine-ish. Rachel came to get me. I was about to ice the top and final tier of the cake."

"Thank you." Rex wished the Pembleton sisters luck with their business and saw them off in their small van. In the dark, he detected two constables guarding the gate.

Back inside the front door, he contemplated the sparsely inhabited hall, which the caterers had cleared of debris and glasses. Roger Litton had ordered take-out from a local Indian restaurant, and his wife and Helen were clearing a space on the table in the great hall. It was beginning to turn decidedly chilly, with only one fireplace to heat the vast space, the other, where the miniature figures had been dug out, having not been relit. He approached Dudley while Mabel was busy cooing over Timmy in a far corner.

"What is Donna's mobile number?"

"She doesn't have one, does she? I already told Freckle Face."

"What about your mother-in-law's number?"

Dudley read the number from his phone. Rex checked it against the digits on his display screen and sighed in frustration. A match. Donna had not called from a pay phone after all. Curious ... Good thing PC Perrin had gone round to Donna's mother's house.

"It's a land line number," Dudley told him. "Susan doesn't have a mobile either, which is just as well, seeing as how much time she and Donna already spend nattering on the phone."

"How much do you owe your bookie?"

"Three thousand quid."

"That extra thousand they're demanding must be interest."

"Norman wouldn't do that. And he'd never send a couple of heavies round. He knows I'm good for it."

"These heavies are threatening to remove Donna's engagement ring by brute force."

"Silly bitch. I told her we should pawn it."

"You don't sound overly concerned."

"Norman wouldn't use those tactics. He's a decent bloke at heart."

"You'd better hope so. 'We know where to find you, Mr. Dudley,'" Rex said in a threatening tone. "Do those words sound familiar to you?"

Dudley chuckled. "That's one of my mates, putting on that voice for a laugh. I saved that message from years ago. It was my stag night. Dave called before they came to pick me up in a limo to take us all to a club in Derby."

"Did a girl jump out of a cake?"

"Yeah, a cake shaped like a hot tub. My boss arranged it." A reminiscing grin spread over Dudley's coarsely handsome features. "My mates did me proud."

"Talking of cakes, did you poison Victoria and Polly Newcombe?"

Caught off guard, as was Rex's intention, Dudley's head snapped up and he gaped at Rex. "What, murder my own—"

"Your own what, Mr. Thorpe?"

"Family. They're my family now that Timmy's wed Polly."

Rex considered all this while scrutinizing the young man.

"What, you don't believe me?" Dudley demanded, his dark gaze glued to Rex's in bold defiance.

"Were you at Newcombe Court before the wedding ceremony?"

"No, I had some business to attend to."

Rex moved on to his next question. "Mr. Thorpe, are you allergic to cats?"

Dudley stared at him in disbelief. "What do you want to know that for?"

"Are you?"

"Well, yeah," the young man said cautiously. "I can't go into my mum's house without sneezing."

"Have you been here all evening?"

"Never left. Ask anybody."

"Somebody was at your mother's tonight. Was it one of your friends?"

Dudley said nothing.

"Come on, Mr. Thorpe. The proverbial cat is out of the bag. Did you tell your friend where to find the key and to go into your old room to remove something that might incriminate you if the police search the house?"

The young man stared back at Rex, clearly wondering how the Scotsman knew so much. "Nothing criminal, I can tell you that much. I've done nothing wrong."

"Doesna mean you're not responsible," Rex told him. "What does Dave look like?"

"Sort of powerful across the shoulders. He's into bodybuilding."

"Does he own a hooded jacket?"

"Now you mention it, yeah. A navy blue one."

"Has he ever been to Newcombe Court?"

"No, never. Why should he?"

Good question, Rex thought. Jasmina may well have been lying about the hooded intruder. "Could one of your friends have told Donna the amount you owed your bookie?"

"My mates are loyal. They'd never tell Donna my private business." So his friends were entitled to know Dudley's private business, but not his wife? "But Timmy might've told her," Dudley added slowly, his jaw slipping askew in suspicion. "I went to him for the three grand, but he said he needed to be saving money now that he had a baby on the way. That's a laugh."

Rex was prevented from probing deeper by Mabel's arrival.

"We're going home now," she told Rex. "Timmy has to rest and Dudley needs to see his boys before they go to bed."

"Susan has the kids tonight," Dudley told her without explaining the circumstances. Presumably he didn't want his mother knowing about the ransom demand.

"I'm afraid I'm going to have to ask you all to stay a while longer until my sergeant returns from Worley," Inspector Lucas intervened, approaching the Thorpe family.

"What's in Worley?" Dudley asked.

"Another dead body," the inspector informed him. "Thomas Newcombe. I wanted the facts before making the announcement."

The Thorpes stared at him, speechless.

"I think you'll find Donna's call was a hoax," Rex told Lucas in private. "She called from her mother's house, not a pay phone."

"As if we wouldn't check."

"She can't have thought her plan through very carefully. I suppose she'll change her story and say her abductors told her to say she was calling from a pay phone so the police wouldn't go straight round to her mum's and apprehend them. Another reason to disbelieve her story: Dudley identified a so-called threatening phone message as being a practical joke by one of his friends on his stag night."

"And you believe him?"

"In retrospect, I do. The message addressed him as Mr. Dudley rather than Mr. Thorpe, which seemed odd."

"I suspected a hoax when her abductors wouldn't come to the phone. PC Perrin will find out more, but it's a ruddy waste of police time. If the ransom turns out to be a scheme of Donna Thorpe's invention, she'll be charged with extortion, no two ways about it."

"She's under severe stress," Rex offered in her defense.

The inspector, who had developed purplish swags beneath his eyes over the course of the evening, looked to be under considerable stress himself. Rex felt partly to blame. If he hadn't gone to Donna's house, she might not have concocted this scam. Perhaps she had just needed a sympathetic ear to begin with, and a desperate plan had evolved after he had witnessed the intruder at Mabel's house.

"She's strung out looking after two wee monsters," Rex went on to explain. "And money is tight."

"Well, her husband shouldn't be frittering it away on the horses. What's she like, this Donna?"

"An ordinary enough lass. She feels trapped, I think, and she's under the impression her husband might have murdered the Newcombes."

191

"Really. And why would she think that?"

Suspecting Donna's motives at the time, Rex had hesitated to tell the inspector about Dudley's absence from the house that morning. He did so now, but urged caution. "If Donna fabricated her own kidnapping, her active imagination is equally capable of framing her husband out of spite. She might even believe he is the murderer. Either way, the hoax appears to be a desperate ploy to get the money owed, plus a bonus for her, before he's arrested."

At that juncture, Sergeant Dartford returned, his squat figure making a beeline for Lucas. One look at his face told Rex he had important news.

"Well?" the inspector asked. "Did you bring the note?

"I have a copy right here." Dartford whipped the item from his pocket with a smug grin. Rex wondered if he had in fact had his teeth knocked in at some point or if it was some genetic defect that made them grow inward and crooked. "The original is being tested for prints."

Lucas read the note and handed it to Rex. "It was found in Newcombe's briefcase. The paper had been torn from the top half of a white sheet. On it were handwritten the words, "*Worley Station Bridge, 9:15 am. M.*"

"What's this smudge at the bottom?" Lucas asked Dartford, leaning into Rex and jabbing at the paper.

"Heavy grease or engine oil on the original. The lab is doing an analysis."

"No envelope?"

"None was found."

Rex addressed the inspector. "May I compare it to the note written to Polly's aunt Gwen asking her to meet the sender at the top of the tower?"

Lucas pulled the plastic-covered missive from his jacket pocket. "I'll have Perrin get this to the lab pronto. Nobody I asked recognized or admitted to recognizing the writing."

"Similar," Rex said, studying the notes. "Spiky capital *M* in both." He jabbed at the first letter of the note to Gwen Jones: "*Meet me at the top of the tower. An admirer.*"

"Perhaps someone should speak to Mack Simmons, the mechanic who was seeing Polly before he moved to St. Ives," Rex suggested. "It might be helpful to corroborate when he left."

Lucas nodded curtly. "It's possible he snuck back. All I got from the guests was that he was an unsavory character who worked at a garage in Aston, which has since closed."

"Robert Carter paid him to leave Aston," Rex told him.

"Hear that?" Lucas asked the sergeant. "I knew that solicitor was hiding something. What else did you find out at Worley?"

"Newcombe fell from one of them wrought-iron bridges with low railings built before suicide and murder became so popular," Dartford replied. "It's only a small station. Platform was deserted around 9:15, according to the ticket clerk. One witness recalls a middle-aged man in a suit up on the bridge, looking as if he was waiting for someone. Could be our man, although middle-aged blokes in suits isn't a rare sight."

"More so on a Saturday," Rex pointed out. "But no one saw the person he was waiting for? No one saw him fall?"

Dartford shook his head emphatically. "No security cameras either. A couple of female shoppers waiting for the next train into

Derby saw the body on the far tracks, split seconds before a fast train went ploughing over it. The briefcase was recovered beside the tracks, intact. It contained his passport, driving licence, family photos, a hotel receipt, and other documentation enabling us to retrace his most recent movements."

Sergeant Dartford proceeded to fill the inspector in on the scant details he had gleaned from his inquiries into Tom Newcombe's life, latterly spent on his common-law wife's family farm outside Bucharest, fixing clocks and watches, and trading in antiques. The woman, Tereza, had been forthcoming about her relationship with Newcombe past and present when visited by the Romanian police, but had denied knowledge of his plans involving a reunion with his daughter beyond the newspaper clipping she had found in a drawer of a desk he was in the process of restoring. He had told her he was going to London on business.

"Seems he lied out of both sides of his mouth," the inspector remarked when Dartford came to the end of his report.

"A shady character, to be sure," the sergeant agreed.

"But how did he get hold of the clipping about his daughter's engagement?" Lucas tapped on his bottom teeth with his pencil.

"Romania is part of the European Union," Dartford reminded his superior. "*The Times* would be available for ex-pats and visitors."

"Maybe *M* sent it to him," Rex ventured.

Lucas told his sergeant to contact Mack Simmons in Cornwall. "If *M* is our murderer," he said, "it can only be one of three people. Let's find out which one."

AFTER A QUICK BOWL of lukewarm curry and a few poppadoms, Rex decided to have another stab at Dudley Thorpe while Dartford was calling St. Ives. Preoccupied with the Worley murder, Lucas had not yet informed Dudley that his wife might have been making the story up about the kidnappers.

Undeterred by the mute hostility Rex felt directed at him from the young man, he sat opposite him and leaned forward, hands clasped loosely between his knees. "I wonder if I might have a few more minutes of your time."

"I've told you and your police friends everything relevant to my wife's situation and to the murder enquiry. And now we're stuck here even longer on account of Mr. Newcombe's death. I'm losing count, mate. And I told you—I have nothing relevant to add."

"Well, it can be hard to know what is relevant," Rex submitted. "For example, what if I were to tell you that Timmy is not the father of Polly's baby?"

"What?" Dudley asked, jolted upright on the sofa. "Whose is it, then?"

"Yours."

"Not true!"

Rex knew Donna wasn't stupid and would have at some time come up with an explanation for the check to Dr. Forspaniak in Derby. Why else would her husband have written out a large amount of money to a gynecologist without her knowledge?

"I think your wife may have an inkling about the baby," Rex told Dudley. "PC Perrin is looking into her kidnapping, but it's possible Donna may have concocted the story to get back at you."

"Wouldn't surprise me."

"I'm assuming Polly refused to have an abortion and you never confessed to your brother the baby was yours."

"Prove it. We're twins."

"Not identical, only fraternal, so paternity could be proved. What if Timmy was incapable of producing a child due to complications from mumps in adolescence?"

Dudley stared at him dumbfounded. "How do you know?"

"It's not how I know that matters as much as who else knows."

"He has one atrophied testicle, but that wouldn't make him completely impotent."

"Why was Timmy not inoculated against mumps?"

"He was ill at the time. And then he contracted mumps when he was fourteen, and he became really ill. That's when our mum got him Monty, because Timmy was contagious and couldn't leave the house. I was immune as I'd had my jabs. How did you find out about the baby?"

Rex could not tell him about the scribble in his son's medical records noting the necessity for a MMR vaccine, "*viz. TPT*"—in other words, referencing Timothy P. Thorpe, the child's uncle, who'd had serious complications from mumps. Nor could he divulge the doctor's telltale expression of surprise regarding Polly's pregnancy.

"It started with a hunch," was all Rex told Dudley. "That item you sent Dave to retrieve, is it something that could point to you as the dad?"

Dudley swore to himself and slumped back on the sofa. His white shirt sleeves were rolled up, darkly matted forearms culminating in strong, tanned hands and, Rex noted with interest, healthy pink nails growing out of perfect half moons.

"It meant nothing for either of us," Dudley said in a hoarse voice as a tremor rippled across his shoulders. "She was on the rebound from Mack Simmons. It was just a bit of fun."

A bit of fun with fatal consequences? Rex wondered. "What were you hiding at your mother's house?"

"A letter, if you must know. From Polly."

"Do young people still write letters?" Rex asked with a measure of surprise.

"She sent a copy of the ultrasound with it. She said she couldn't get rid of the baby once she'd seen it. I'd offered to pay for a termination even though I wasn't entirely sure it was mine."

"And you kept the letter and ultrasound. Sentimental reasons?"

Dudley slid back further into the sofa and leaned his head on the backrest, staring up into the open pyramid of the ceiling. "I don't know why I kept them. I suppose it felt wrong to throw something like that out with the rubbish. I couldn't keep them at

197

my house; Donna likes to snoop. There's a space under the floor-boards in my old room where I used to hide stuff growing up."

"Do your mates know that Polly's baby is yours?"

"No chance. And Dave won't peek. The envelope's sealed. He doesn't know what it's about. No one knows except Polly and me. And she wouldn't tell anyone, least of all her mother who hates me—hated me—and her blabbermouth friend Amber."

"Who's in love with you."

Dudley grimaced. "I wouldn't get with that ugly chick if she was the last woman on earth."

Rex stifled a harsh response to the man's callousness. "Polly didn't want to hurt her best friend by confiding she was having an affair with you, and she couldn't risk her mother finding out. She led Amber to believe she was still seeing Simmons behind her mother's back. But it will no doubt be confirmed shortly that he moved to Cornwall in the middle of September, which means he can't be the baby's father."

"Well, maybe it's someone else's."

"I think you know that's not the case."

"What's going to happen now?" Dudley asked in a tone which conveyed a calm sense of fatality.

"The final act," Rex replied. "And then the curtain will come down."

"On who?" Dudley asked grimly.

DARTFORD CROSSED TO INSPECTOR Lucas in perplexed excitement. Leaving Dudley anxiously brooding, Rex joined them in time to hear the sergeant recount his telephone conversation with Mack Simmons.

"He moved to St. Ives on the thirteenth of September and hasn't been out of Cornwall since," Dartford stressed. "He's been busy setting up shop and got married meantime. Simmons said Carter had made it quite clear he was never to return to Aston, and he had no desire to anyway. Said he's happy with his missus, has a child on the way, and business is ticking over very nicely, thank you." The sergeant closed his notebook. "Mack Simmons bears no grudges, says the windfall was a blessing. I don't think he's our *M*."

He wasn't the father of Polly's baby either, Rex added to himself. Dr. Williamitis had confirmed her due date as late June, by then making it nine and a half months since Carter had run Mack Simmons out of town.

"With Simmons out of the picture, my guess is the grease spot on the note is something Newcombe used to oil the clocks he worked on," the inspector said. "That would suggest he received the letter at his home in Romania."

"No mail to his London hotel," the sergeant corroborated. "No calls either—I checked," he pre-empted Lucas, who had opened his mouth to speak. "And he didn't own a laptop, so—"

"There is one other person whose name begins with *M* that we know was at Worley Station this morning," Lucas interjected. "Meredith Matthews. Plus she was in the reception room taking care of the victims around the time the figures went missing from the cake." The inspector turned to Dartford. "We should question her again. She seems pretty sharp, that one. And she's been keeping a low profile, as has her boyfriend."

"Meredith has no motive that I can see," Rex countered. "In any case, the body was on the tracks before her train arrived. Mabel Thorpe, our third *M*, is a more likely suspect. She's no stranger to arsenic."

"Why would Mabel Thorpe want to kill her own grandchild?" the inspector asked doubtfully.

"'Aye, there's the rub,' to quote Hamlet," as Rex frequently did, since murder mystery cases made for a quantity of doubt and indecision, especially this one. "But if poor wee Timmy was cuckolded..."

"Oh, enough of the Elizabethan twaddle, Graves," the inspector exclaimed with an irritable shake of his container of aspirin. "The case is complicated enough in plain English."

"Mabel seems devoted to her other two grand-bairns, but she may have known that Polly's child was not Timmy's," Rex said in plain Scottish.

"It's not? Oh ruddy hell," the inspector responded glumly. "This case is murkier than a cesspit. Whose is it, then?"

"Dudley's. He admitted as much."

"There's a lot pointing to Dudley. But if Mabel Thorpe knew the baby was Dudley's, she still wouldn't want to poison it, would she?"

"She may be laboring under the misapprehension that the child is Mack Simmons'. Everyone knew about Polly and Mack."

"It's all circumstantial," Lucas lamented. "The most incriminating evidence is the letter *M*. I'd like a bit more to go on. Have everyone submit a sample of their handwriting using phrases from the two notes," he instructed his sergeant. "That'll test the culprit's nerves. If it can be proved Mabel was the messenger in both cases, we have our murderer, or at least a co-conspirator."

"It is possible Newcombe was in contact with the groom's mother," Dartford acknowledged, absently scratching the root of a cauliflower ear. "He may've wanted to find out the lie of the land before barging back into his first family's lives."

"Why not contact his sister?"

"Gwen told me he hadn't been in touch with her in ten years," Rex supplied. "And from what I gather, she wasn't in constant contact with the Newcombe family."

Lucas gave the orange splodges on his face a vigorous rub. "According to the catering staff, Mabel Thorpe arrived at Newcombe Court at eight to help out with preparations for the reception and left shortly after nine to meet the aunt at Derby Station at 9:45.

That gave her enough time to meet Newcombe off his 9:15 train at Worley first."

"Even if she was late reaching Derby Station, Gwen wasn't on the train anyway, so nobody was the wiser," Rex contributed.

"Get the remaining guests to write both right and left-handed," Lucas directed the sergeant. "One by one in the kitchen. Hopefully we'll have more success with the writing samples than with the photos. Shame no one shot a consecutive video of the latter part of the reception."

Rex joined the guests from Polly's old school. Clive had left some time earlier with his tail between his legs after protesting his ignorance of Jasmina's involvement in the crimes. Helen was dozing on a fireside sofa next to Diana Litton, who flashed a fuchsia smile at him. Of those present, she seemed the least affected by the drawn-out investigation.

"Getting anywhere?" she asked.

"We may have an answer soon." He sat down in a wing armchair beside Roger Litton's.

"No good deed goes unpunished," Diana's bald-headed husband proffered peevishly. "I wish I hadn't agreed to escort the Welsh woman partway up the steps. That makes me a person of interest in the case. Most of the other guests got to go home."

Rex rifled through his notes, reminded of something. *The fat one in the floaty mauve dress*, as the DJ had described Aunt Gwen in answer to his question about whether he had seen a short, dark-haired woman going up the tower steps. Harry's reply in the interrogative, which had not fully registered with Rex at the time, implied that he might have seen more than one short, dark-haired woman—

202

the other being Mabel Thorpe. "I wonder," he murmured, chewing thoughtfully on the cardboard corner of his notebook cover.

"What do you wonder?" Helen murmured, coming out of her doze.

"How would you describe Mabel Thorpe?"

His fiancée stretched and yawned. "Short, middle-aged brunette."

"And Gwendolyn Jones?"

"The same, but rounder."

"Exactly so." The DJ might have seen both women enter the stairwell at around the crucial time. Rex spun his pencil in the air and caught it adroitly. Helen eyed him with suspicion and, arranging herself more comfortably against the sofa cushions, closed her lids.

"You were probably the last person to see her alive before she met her killer at the top of the tower," Rex told Litton.

"Yes, I know," the teacher agonized. "If I'd gone all the way up I would have seen the murderer, and Polly's aunt might still be alive." He mopped his shiny dome with a red polka-dot handkerchief. "But, hang it all, I'm sick and tired of all the police interviews. We've been sitting here for hours."

"Not much longer, Roger," his wife consoled him.

Rex didn't have the heart to tell them about the writing test in store. The sergeant had already rounded up the family members. "Diana, when you mentioned the Borgias earlier and referred to arsenic being called 'inheritance powder,' it made me think of Mithridates."

Helen moaned in her sleep. She didn't open her eyes. He directed his attention back to the history teacher, who had straightened into a more alert posture on the sofa.

"Did it now?" she said approvingly. "And what can you tell me about the ancient king of Pontus?"

"That he was paranoid about being poisoned by claimants to his throne and had slaves taste his food. He concocted an antidote made out of honey, and if I'm not mistaken—"

"You are never mistaken," Helen mumbled, apparently not asleep after all.

"This is going back to my early school days," Rex informed Diana Litton. "But I seem to remember that the wily old king is credited with having tried to acquire immunity to poisoning by building up a tolerance to it."

Diana extended her hands in quiet applause. "Very good, Rex. You must have a phenomenal retentive memory."

"Like an elephant," Helen remarked placidly from the cushions.

"Why are we discussing ancient history?" Roger Litton demanded querulously.

"We're trying to establish who might have been immune to the arsenic introduced into the cake," Rex explained. "The only people who ate the top tier and didn't end up in hospital were Mabel Thorpe and her son."

"Timmy was sick," Diana pointed out.

"Aye, enough to avert suspicion. Mabel may have just pretended to eat the cake, but chances are she had some."

"Where would she have procured arsenic?"

"Possibly from her late husband's supply. He had been taking it as a cure of last resort for his leukemia. My suspicion is Mabel Thorpe laced her morning tea with it, and Timmy's as well."

This was as reasonable an explanation as any for why Mabel had hand-washed the cups, saucers and tea spoons while the rest of the breakfast items had been left in the dishwasher.

"Timmy can't have been in on the plot to murder his wife and child," Diana insisted. "I simply cannot believe it of him. He worships Polly."

"I never saw such a mismatched pair," Roger Litton remarked. "Polly is fun and spontaneous, Timmy so serious. Attraction of opposites, do you suppose?"

"But if Mabel Thorpe wanted Timmy to inherit Newcombe Court," Litton's wife asked Rex, "why not just murder Tom and Victoria Newcombe? And, I suppose, Aunt Gwen, for good measure?"

"That, Diana, was the stumbling block in the Mabel theory until I made a few discoveries."

"Well, I hope all will be revealed soon," the history teacher said when no further information was forthcoming. She sighed softly. "Perhaps it's just as well Tom Newcombe didn't make it to the wedding. What a shock it would have been to see his estranged wife and daughter poisoned and his sister's skull crushed on the back patio. Any news on Polly and the baby's progress?"

"Not since Timmy reported the baby was in stable condition."

"That's one piece of good news for Timmy."

Until he gets the news about whose baby it actually is, Rex thought. Now for the fireworks.

REX WAS ITCHING TO confront Mabel Thorpe. However, it was not his place to do so, aside from which, much of his information had been gathered outside the official scope of the police investigation. And so he waited impatiently while Mrs. Thorpe completed the writing test in the kitchen vacated by the caterers. In the meantime, he wandered about the great hall attempting to form a cohesive picture with the disparate parts assembled in the case.

At last, Sergeant Dartford followed Mabel out of the second wing, ready to call the next person. Rex caught his eye and raised his eyebrows in question. Dartford responded with a curt shake of his head. Negative result.

"She may just be adept at disguising her writing," Lucas said, appearing at Rex's elbow.

"Her driving licence. That'll have her signature on it."

"Good thinking. Wait here."

Lucas returned with the polycarbonate photocard showing Mabel's digitally reproduced signature on it. "Well, what do you know? Spiky capital *M*, as on the anonymous notes. Similar, anyway."

Rex studied it carefully and concurred, just as Dartford was rounding up Roger Litton. Lucas motioned his sergeant over to their side of the hall.

"Suspend further testing for now," he directed. "We have a suspect in the writing of the two notes." He held the photocard up to Dartford.

"That's good news," the sergeant said. "I wasn't getting very far with the writing samples."

In unison, and without further discussion, the three of them went to accost Mabel. The inspector returned her license with his thanks and asked her sons to permit him and his colleagues a few minutes in private with their mother. Dudley got up from the sofa reluctantly, Timmy meekly. When they had left, the men sat in a semicircle surrounding her chair, where she sat primly with her beige cloche hat resting on her knees.

"You are not under arrest," the inspector assured her with benign, freckled charm. "However, the signature on your driving licence bears a resemblance to the writing on the note in Thomas Newcombe's briefcase. We wondered if perhaps you were in communication with him."

"I was not. I never knew him."

"You left Newcombe Court this morning just after nine to collect Gwendolyn Jones from the station in Derby."

"That is correct. Victoria Newcombe was busy getting ready for the wedding ceremony, so I offered to go."

How convenient, thought Rex. *And you moved Carter's whisky bottles to create a diversion while you tampered with the cake before leaving for the station.*

"You stopped off at Worley Station first," the inspector pursued.

"Why would I do that?" Mabel asked with a plausible show of surprise.

"To bring Mr. Newcombe to the church service and reception?"

"I have already told you, I didn't know him."

"You didn't know Mrs. Jones and yet you went to pick her up from the station."

"She was expected. As far as I know, nobody knew Mr. Newcombe was attending his daughter's wedding, unless it was a closely kept secret, meant to surprise Polly."

"Somebody knew," Lucas told her.

Mabel looked around the room. Timmy was helping himself to coffee from the urn and had his back to her. Dudley, however, was watching the proceedings intently from where he sprawled in a distant armchair.

Lucas gave a hesitant cough, and Rex guessed what was coming next.

"Supposing the baby is not Timmy's—" The inspector leveled his blue gaze upon Mabel.

What little color remained in her face suddenly leached out of it. "What do you mean?"

The inspector turned to Rex.

"Timmy contracted mumps as an adolescent," Rex obliged.

Anger put the color back in her cheeks. "How did you get hold of that information?"

"The mumps got me thinking. You would never knowingly murder your own grandchild."

"Of course I wouldn't! What are you talking about?"

"Calm down, Mrs. Thorpe," Lucas instructed and continued. "You nursed your husband through his leukemia. You were uniquely qualified to add the arsenic used in his treatment to the icing when Stella Pembleton was called out of the kitchen this morning."

Mabel stared at him, her skin a bright crimson.

"After the victims were taken away in the ambulance and the reception room was cleared, you snuck in there to get rid of the evidence. Someone saw you go in," he bluffed.

"I went in to air the room, which was fetid."

Now Rex knew for sure she was lying. "I had already opened the window," he informed her. "You removed the miniature bride and groom from the cake and threw them into the fireplace. You disposed of the foil base somewhere and hid the leftover cake crumbs and icing in the dovecote up on the tower roof in the hope birds would eat them so no trace would be left. I'd bet my last Guinness those remains contain the arsenic we've been looking for."

Lucas dispatched Dartford with a brusque sweep of the hand. "SOCO probably collected them, but check anyway." The sergeant shambled off toward the spiral stairway in evident reluctance.

"I further suspect that crumbs will be found in your pocket," Rex resumed.

"Please remove your jacket," the inspector directed Mabel.

She did so and, snapping on a pair of latex gloves, Lucas carefully turned out the pockets of her beige suit, where tiny crumbs and icing stuck to the lining. He scraped them up for analysis. "What are crumbs doing in your pocket?" he asked.

"I wanted to feed the birds."

"Up on the tower?"

"No, I was never on the tower. I threw the crumbs out the downstairs window for the sparrows. I didn't know they had arsenic on them."

"The DJ saw you go up the stone steps," Rex informed her.

"He must be mistaken. He didn't strike me as being particularly bright."

Rex had to give her credit. Mabel Thorpe was nobody's fool. Wringing a confession out of her was not going to prove easy. He ploughed on, so as not to lose momentum, in the hope she would trip herself up under the unrelenting pressure.

"Inconveniently, Aunt Gwen did not eat the cake, so you fabricated a note from an admirer. Imagine her surprise when she sees you at the top of the tower instead. Harder to imagine how you got her up on the parapet. Did your hat pin provide the necessary threat? Is that what you used on Tom Newcombe?"

"These accusations are insane!" She turned to Inspector Lucas for support, but received no sympathy from that quarter, only a severe expression of rebuke.

"Once you found out Mr. Newcombe was alive, you had to add him to your death list. Now that Timmy was marrying into money, you saw a chance to live a life of ease and help Dudley out of his financial difficulties. You brought charcoal tablets to help absorb the poison, having warned Timmy not to eat more than a tiny morsel of cake since he was suffering from what he termed a 'funny tummy.' Incidentally, do you routinely carry charcoal tablets around in your handbag?"

Mabel's impassive face gave nothing away. "I do. It's good for stomach upsets."

"And just to be sure, you've been trying to inure him from arsenic poisoning by feeding him small doses over a period of time."

"I never."

"Mrs. Thorpe, Timmy exhibits outward physical signs of chronic exposure," Rex said, lightly dismissing her outrage. "His nails, for example. Dudley, you knew, would not touch the cake. You didn't care about Mrs. Newcombe, Polly, or even the baby, which you suspected wasn't Timmy's and didn't know was Dudley's."

"It can't be!"

"The child is, indeed, his."

Mabel jumped to her feet. "You're lying." She spun around wildly. "Is it true?" she screamed at Dudley. "Is Polly's baby yours? Why didn't you tell me?"

Dudley just stared at her, as if her current reaction were reason enough. Helen, Carter, and the Littons sat up in their seats while Meredith and Reggie watched the drama from a secluded sofa.

"What is she going on about?" Timmy asked no one in particular, the cup of coffee he was holding rattling in its saucer.

Inspector Lucas approached him and put a hand on his shoulder, preparing to lead him away and, Rex assumed, give him the bad news about Polly's baby. Shrugging the inspector off, Timmy handed him the cup of coffee and strode over to his brother.

"You bastard," he cried, pulling Dudley out of his armchair by the collar. They stood glaring at each other. Timmy had the advantage of blind rage.

"It meant nothing, I swear!" his twin entreated.

"Stop it. Stop it!" Mabel cried out, but not before Dudley received a blow from his brother that knocked him back in his chair. She flew to Dudley's side while Timmy stared at his fist in amazement and flexed his fingers to make sure nothing was broken.

"I dare say you had reason to strike your brother, Timmy," his mother said, kneeling on the rug and dabbing at Dudley's cut lip with a paper napkin. "But I warned you against marrying that slut."

"It's none of your business. You had no right to interfere!"

"Such ingratitude! Everything I've done has been for you and your brother."

"You forced me to drink tea every morning, which you said was fortified with vitamins, and all the time I felt sicker. Were you trying to kill me?"

"Of course not. I was trying to protect you from a poisoner. That's what I've always done! Taken care of you."

"Was Dudley in on this plot to get rid of the Newcombes?" Rex asked, attacking her Achilles' heel—her sons.

"No! Dudley didn't know I'd kept his father's Trisenox."

There it was. In her anxiety to protect Dudley, she had confessed to the arsenic.

"Mother, are you stark raving mad?" Timmy lunged at her, but Rex stepped into his path.

"Timmy, I believe your mother thought the baby was Mack Simmons' but waited to do anything until after the wedding, when she was assured of your future at Newcombe Court."

"I don't care about Newcombe Court. Polly's the only girl who ever loved me!"

Inspector Lucas set down Timmy's coffee cup.

"Mrs. Thorpe," he addressed Mabel in a solemn voice that belied the glow of satisfaction in his pale blue eyes. "I'm arresting you on suspicion of murder in the deaths of Reverend Alfred Snood, Gwendolyn Newcombe Jones, Thomas Newcombe, Victoria Newcombe, and the attempted murder of Polly Newcombe and her unborn child."

"A PRODUCTIVE DAY'S WORK," Inspector Lucas congratulated himself after his sergeant had recalled PC Perrin from Aston and taken Mabel Thorpe into custody, the suspect protesting her innocence and admitting only to having had arsenic in her possession at home. Her two sons left shortly thereafter, as did the Littons and Bobby Carter, who wanted to be by Polly's bedside with Timmy.

"I felt sure Carter was implicated," the inspector told Rex, hovering by the portcullis door, on the point of departure.

"Whether he helped Tom Newcombe disappear, we may never know," Rex replied.

"One thing for sure, Mabel Thorpe will never benefit from her crimes. Even if she retracts her confession about the arsenic, which she says was stolen from her house, we have the crumb samples found on her person, the notes which an expert can compare with her writing, and the hat pin, conforming to the instrument used in the murder of Thomas Newcombe."

"She vehemently denies murdering the victims," Rex said, playing devil's advocate.

"Why did she keep the arsenic after her husband died? Rather irresponsible, if you ask me. She must've thought it might come in handy one day. Timmy Thorpe is heartbroken over his mother. Showed spunk when he turned on his brother."

"Not surprisingly. Dudley deceived his wife as well. I can only imagine the reception he'll get when he arrives home. Will you drop the charges against Donna?"

Lucas sighed magnanimously. "Staging your own kidnapping in an attempt to extort money is a serious business, but no one got hurt, and you say she was helpful in the investigation."

"She was the one who told me about the arsenic used in Dr. Thorpe's cancer treatment, and she provided me with the first clue that her husband might be Polly's father."

When Rex had spoken to Dr. Williamitis on the phone and discovered that the canceled check hidden at Mabel's house might be for a termination, he remembered the argument Jasmina had said she witnessed between Dudley and Polly—apparently a lovers' tiff.

Rex and Lucas took leave of each other. It had been a long and eventful night, and Rex was beginning to feel how the inspector looked—drawn and frayed. He rounded up Helen and their young houseguests.

"Some wedding," Reggie said, exiting the front door.

The rain, Rex was pleased to see, had stopped.

"Are you sure you still want to get married?" he asked Helen on the way to the car.

"What are you getting at, Rex?" she asked, blue eyes narrowing at him. "Are you getting cold feet?"

215

"Och, no!" He decided this wasn't the moment to admit that he was. "I just mean, well, as far as weddings go, this one was a bit of a disaster, don't you think?"

"You could call multiple murders a disaster," she agreed.

"I suppose now we'll have to go to the funerals." It was the respectful thing to do, after all. Rex wondered if he could get away with wearing the same suit.

Helen looked at him strangely. "That's all right, dear. I think it might be better if I attend the funerals by myself. Murder seems to have a habit of turning up whenever you're around."

Rex couldn't argue with that fact, and didn't try.

The four of them piled into the blue car, Helen at the wheel.

"I wonder if the Malt Shovel in Aston is still serving bar food," Rex said. "It's got a comfortable lounge."

"How do you know?" Helen asked, pulling her seat belt over her shoulder.

"I was there this evening for the purpose of research. A local from the village knew about Tom Newcombe's affair with the Romanian au pair." Rex was curious to see if old Jessop had been allowed back into the establishment. "In any case, it's a fine old pub. Definitely worth a visit."

"Or, in your case—two," Helen said dryly. "And I'll just bet the beer is good."

"Fine ales, and cider for you."

"Oh, all right then. You've managed to twist my arm. Okay with you two?" she asked the young couple in the back, who responded enthusiastically.

"Don't care if I never see that horror again," Meredith said with a backward glance at Newcombe Court as they took off down the driveway lined with statues shining ethereally in the gloom. "None of this might've happened if Polly hadn't tried to hide the truth about the baby."

"She didn't know her uncle Bobby had paid Simmons off," Rex explained. "But if she suspected her mother of having had something to do with his disappearance, she may have kept the truth about Dudley and the baby from her out of spite. Or shame."

"So she decided to palm the baby off on Timmy," Helen took over the narrative. "Victoria was happy that her daughter had finally settled down. Everyone was happy, except Mabel. Seems she was not going to let Polly ruin her son's life, but nor was she going to pass up the opportunity of a lifetime. Once Timmy was married into the Newcombe family, he stood to inherit a modest fortune— once a few people were out of the way. And what better time to eliminate the other side of the family than at the wedding?"

"Tom Newcombe, eager for a reconciliation with his daughter, agreed to the rendezvous at Worley Station," Rex pursued, gazing out of the passenger window at the dark countryside. "Returning for the first time from Romania, Worley was his fatal destination. A hat pin through the heart and he fell over the bridge. The attack proved efficacious enough for Mabel to repeat it later at the top of the tower. Evidently, she did not anticipate Polly's tenacious hold on life. But for Polly and the baby, she would have succeeded in her mission to eradicate all Newcombe blood."

"So sad for Polly," Meredith lamented. "I wonder how Madonna will feel about Dudley's illegitimate child. She and Polly used to be best friends."

"Madonna?" Rex queried.

"She goes by Donna now, but back in school she was Madonna. We had the same initials: Meredith Matthews and Madonna Maddox. Her mum was a big Madonna fan, had all her albums and dressed just like her, which embarrassed Donna no end."

Rex recalled the fake diamond studs in Susan's ear. "I see," he said, beginning, indeed, to see what he had missed. Now all the pieces tumbled neatly into place.

When the car reached the pub, he told Helen and their young guests to go ahead and order, explaining he had some unfinished business to attend to in the village. As he took off for Donna Thorpe's house, he could feel his blood roiling from having been so roundly had, his good nature taken advantage of by a scheming and vindictive woman, one even more evil in her way than he had supposed Mabel to be.

If ever two people deserved each other, it was Donna and Dudley Thorpe. Theirs had been a marriage made not in heaven but hell.

DONNA THORPE MET REX at the door to her house, a cardigan draped over her shoulders as though she might have been expecting him. "Mr. Graves, how nice to see you again." She looked abashed, and also guarded beneath the porch light. "Have you come about the ransom I tried to pull off? I should never've involved you, but you seemed so kind and sympathetic when you came round earlier that I decided to turn to you, thinking you would help."

Rex felt significantly less sympathetic now. "I've come aboot something more serious. Are your boys home?"

"They're at my mum's."

"And your husband?"

"At Mabel's house with the police. She'll probably be sent to Foston Hall Prison, for life."

"Does that not make you feel just a wee bit guilty?"

"Why should it?"

"Listen, Madonna—"

"Don't call me that! I hate it."

"That's what Mr. Newcombe knew you by though, isn't it? And that's how you signed your note to him: *M*. The game's up, Donna. Why don't you tell me in your own words how you came up with such a clever plan to murder the Newcombe family."

Donna's eyes glowed. "It was a clever plan, wasn't it? And clever of you to suss it out."

"I almost didn't." Luckily, Meredith had inadvertently reverted to Donna's full name, causing the penny to drop. How could he have been so blind? Well, Donna was a skillful liar and an accomplished actress, that's how.

The killer drew the front door closed behind her and huddled under her cardigan. She was not going to invite him inside, but she seemed ready to talk. And he was ready to listen. "When you turned up at my house today looking for answers, I saw a way to frame my husband for the Newcombe murders. For your benefit, I gave him a motive—the gambling debts; means—arsenic; and opportunity—his absence from home this morning. But ultimately Mabel did just as well, and my boys get to keep their dad. Lucky her name begins with *M* too!

"I knew the truth about Polly's baby. A gossip at the pub saw my husband and Polly together. Then, after I first found the cancelled check to Dr. Forspaniak—the one I showed you, and which I knew you'd follow up on, as I had—I put two and two together. One more reason for Dud to get rid of Polly, before the truth came out.

"I snuck out of the house this morning while Dud was out and the boys were at my mum's making the fairy cakes. Borrowing her car, I drove to Newcombe Court. I didn't know what I was going to do with the arsenic at that point but, once again, luck was on my side. No one was in the kitchen and the top tier of the cake hadn't been iced yet. The white icing was still in the mixing bowl.

"My mother-in-law kept an old unused prescription of Trisenox in her sideboard—the stuff the police found. She hoards everything. A few months ago she noticed ampoules were missing and, ever paranoid, must have thought someone might try to poison her or her precious Timmy, so she put a small dose in their morning tea to build up a tolerance and immediately washed out the cups so the cat wouldn't get at it. She never reported the theft to the police. I monitored how much she was using. Timmy showed all the classic symptoms of chronic arsenic poisoning. I wasn't sure how diluted the injectable Trisenox was and I had to be sure it was a fatal dose.

"I sent Tom Newcombe the newspaper clipping announcing his daughter's engagement. My mom kept in touch with Tereza, Polly's nanny, after she returned to Romania. Tereza minded me from time to time with Polly, and my mum sometimes looked after Polly when the nanny had her days off. I hated Mrs. Newcombe for firing her. Polly and I drifted apart over the years, and she outright ignored me after I married Dudley. I realize now she must have always fancied him.

"Anyway, I told Mr. Newcombe how wonderful it would be for him to surprise his daughter on her wedding day. Victoria would forgive him after all these years. She could finally marry Bobby Carter! I didn't think he would bring my note. I had arranged to meet him at Worley Station and came armed with one of Mabel's hat pins. I slipped back to Newcombe later and spied Aunt Gwen through the window refusing the cake. I remembered her from when I used to play at Newcombe Court with Polly. I left a note on the bartender's tray when he was getting ice in the kitchen. A brunette in a silver dress saw me, but nothing came of it, as I was bundled up in a hooded jacket and she probably couldn't give a helpful description. The DJ was busy working on one of his speakers.

"While everyone was toasting the happy pair, I went to the top of the tower and waited for Polly's aunt. I used the hat pin to force her over the edge—wasn't difficult as Gwen was tipsy and woozy from her climb."

Rex nodded pensively. "I was on the right track, but thought at first your mother-in-law had executed the plan. She must have panicked and hidden the crumbs in the dovecote when she realized arsenic had been put in the cake, and she'd be blamed if the poison was traced back to her house. I suppose she got rid of the bride and groom figures for the same reason."

"I really would have liked to have got rid of the whole rotten lot of Newcombes," Donna said with grim wistfulness. "Timmy would have inherited the money, and Dud would have been able to finagle what he needed out of him. When Polly's baby is out of intensive care, Dud wants us to bring it up with our own two, if she's too sick to look after it. That's what he told me on the phone. The nerve!" She sniffed in derision. "Of course, he has no clue what I did and has always said his mother was bonkers."

"And so many accidents can befall a baby, isn't that right, Donna?"

"I wouldn't hurt him now everybody knows he's Dudley's. He's the ticket out of our financial mess, more than Timmy."

"You won't have financial concerns where you're going. Her Majesty's Prison Service will provide adequately for you."

"You're going to turn me in, then?" Donna slumped into a sitting position on the doorstep. "Well, of course you are. But I'm almost too tired to care."

"I called Detective Lucas on my way here. Why, Donna?"

She stared out over the square of damp grass beyond her porch to the glistening road and row of uninspiring houses on the other side. "My wedding was a fairytale. It was perfect, every girl's dream. And then it ended. I spent my time planning the *getting* married part and didn't give enough thought to the *being* married part. I should've listened to my mom. Polly carrying my husband's child down the aisle was the final straw."

"'Those whom God has joined together, let no one put asunder,'" Rex murmured as a police siren replaced the memory of a joyful peal of bells heard at All Saints' Church earlier that day.

An inauspicious day, as Rex had rightly predicted.

THE END

ABOUT THE AUTHOR

Born in Bloomington, Indiana, and now living permanently in Florida, C. S. Challinor was educated in Scotland and England, and holds a joint honors degree in Latin and French from the University of Kent, Canterbury, as well as a diploma in Russian from the Pushkin Institute in Moscow. She has traveled extensively and enjoys discovering new territory for her novels.